# THE CLOACA

BY ANDREW HOOD

Invisible Publishing
Halifax & Toronto

Library and Archives Canada Cataloguing in Publication

Hood, Andrew, 1983-

The cloaca / Andrew Hood.

Short stories.

ISBN 978-1-926743-19-6

I. Title.

PS8615.O511C56 2012 C813'.6 C2012-901541-5

Cover & Interior designed by Megan Fildes

Typeset in Laurentian and Slate by Megan Fildes
With thanks to type designer Rod McDonald

Printed and bound in Canada

Invisible Publishing
Halifax & Toronto
www.invisiblepublishing.com

We acknowledge the support of the Canada Council for the Arts which last year invested $20.1 million in writing and publishing throughout Canada.

Invisible Publishing recognizes the support of the Province of Nova Scotia through the Department of Communities, Culture & Heritage. We are pleased to work in partnership with the Culture Division to develop and promote our cultural resources for all Nova Scotians.

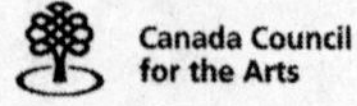


Conseil des Arts
du Canada

For Telly the Woman, and for Teets
Meru and Milo "Gavin" Hopkins.

The best family a guy could ever had.

"Of course all life is a process of breaking down, but the blows that do the dramatic side of the work—the big sudden blows that come, or seem to come, from the outside—the ones you remember and blame things on and, in moments of weakness, tell your friends about, don't show their effect all at once. There is another sort of blow that comes from within—that you don't feel until it's too late to do anything about it, until you realize with finality that in some regard you will never be as good a man again."

–F. Scott Fitzgerald, "The Crack-Up"

"He called the shit *poop*!"

–*Billy Madison*

# MANNING

"I'm gonna hit the can like it hit me first," my mom says. "Man the booth, Pickle." She squats, ducks under the table and pops back up on the other side. Jingling her keys, she disappears down the aisles of other booths.

*Like it hit me first* is one of my mom's classic phrases. She's been using that since I can remember being embarrassed of her. It's an okay one, as far as go-to phrases go: not quite smart and not quite funny, but just enough of both of those to elicit at least a smirk. Unless you've heard the hell out of it, then your mouth screws up another way. "Night, Pickle. I'm gonna hit the hay like it hit me first. Don't stay up too late." "Buckle up, Pickle, and let's hit the road like it hit us first." "I'm not against you drinking, Pickle, but keep in mind how your dad would hit that bottle like it hit him first."

Sean's splitting has inspired a new number in her repertoire. Everything has to be manned all of a sudden. "Man the apartment, Pickle, while I go out for spaghetti sauce." "Man the car, Pickle, while I run in here for a lotto ticket." "Man the basketball, Pickle, while I go see if those two black kids want to play two-on-two." As if this one guy—who even when he was around was never around much—had his finger stuck into a crack in some hypothetical dam. And now that he's hit the road like it hit him first, someone else has to plug that hole so everything doesn't just gush and break through and drown everything else. It's like, "Here, Pickle, man the world while I'm gone, will you?"

While my mom's hitting the can like it hit her first, this big pile of human being comes up to our booth I've been left to man. He's got this mustache on his face, but it doesn't look like a mustache he grew. More like he couldn't grow a beard.

"What've you got?" the pile of human being wants to know. He looks sad about the boxes we've got opened on the table, and a little tired about them. The good burgundy tablecloth that's been in the family since before Christ pissed the bed does not, as my mom insists, help.

"There's some baseball," I tell him. "Some basketball, some hockey. Some of everything. Some cards from Desert Storm are in there, too, I think."

"But what've you *got*?" His eyes look like they've been thumbed into his head, like the sunken coal eyes of a snowman.

"We've got what we've got," I say.

The pile sighs like air escaping from a vinyl chair when it gets sat on. This has to be his first time at this collector's show, to be coming to our booth at all, let alone asking me what we've got. Every month it's the same hoarders and sad sacks and single dads who come, and they all know that my mom and me don't have anything, and that even if we did have anything, we wouldn't know we had it. These limp, sweaty guys come to the booth to flirt with Mom, suck in their guts and maybe buy a card on the off chance that it might improve their chances, but that's about it. You can't improve a chance you don't have.

The last Sunday of every month, for the five-dollar fee, my mom and I set up our pointless booth at The Arena. This place isn't even called The Arena, that's just what it's been dubbed. Where the name was supposed to be there's just a big blank space. For a while there was a weird-looking dick that someone had spray-painted in that spot, so it was known as the Big Green Dick Arena. Another week and someone else climbed up there to add different-coloured nuts to the dick. And later someone even went to the trouble to add curly hair to those balls. But now the space is blank again.

This is the hockey rink that Corbet's OHL team was supposed to kick ass on. I don't know what goes on, whether they melt the ice or just put a flooring over top of it, but there's always a wet chill here and that sweet chemical smell that all indoor rinks have, folded into the reek of locker room. The team this whole facility was built for was going to be called The Corbet Combats and something with a bat was going to be the logo. There was even a competition in The Mercury to design some lame mascot. I don't know if someone down at City Hall bungled the math or what, but the way it worked out was the town had enough money for an OHL team or for an arena, but not for both. So we got the arena for a hockey team, but no hockey team. Now The Arena gets rented out for kids' birthdays, school skating parties, the circus—not the good circus—Neil Diamond that one time, Tom Jones that other, and, every last Sunday of the month, this glorified garage sale.

The pile's got a shoulder bag, one of those cheap-ass ones they give away at conventions, and when he adjusts it I see that his left hand is a little itty claw. The other hand is in okay shape, though something about the little stubby fingers brings baby penises to mind. So with his baby penises he goes through every single card in every single box of Sean's collection. He's one of these guys who needs to find out for himself that we have nothing. And I've got to stand there like I'm listening to someone tell a joke I've heard a million times because this is my booth to man now, my worthless cards to man. And the pile is mine to man now, too.

I get the feeling that in life you're rarely lucky enough to know just where the shit has come from that gets cut up and thrown by the blades of your fan. But I can tell you that all of this is Ben Rooney's fault. Ben Rooney was this guy Sean worked nights with at the chainsaw factory who just disappeared one day. What happened was Ben Rooney sold his lifelong baseball card collection for a million dollars apparently and then hit the road like it had hit him first. A wife and daughter were left behind. I knew Claire Rooney. She went to the same school as me for a few years, though this was before her dad scrammed. She was that girl who in kindergarten would come in from recess during the winter and, starting with her snowsuit, take off all her clothes, all the way down to her doll body. Her dad was never heard from again, though I heard about him all the time, because fucking Ben Rooney became this big hero for Sean. And that's the source of this huge load of elephant dook that got chucked at my fan and sprayed pretty much all over everything.

"I swear to God," Sean started saying. "A million dollars." Like swearing to God meant anything. Swearing to God for him was just the same as saying "excuse me" in the tail end of the belch he'd sneak up and put in my ear.

With dollar signs twinkling in his eyes, Sean started buying baseball cards like rations before a disaster. In his mind this was as good as buying money. Seriously: like buying fucking money. Like he was going out and paying one dollar for ten dollars. That's what he'd figured out from that Ben Rooney story. I would never ask Mom what on earth she was doing with such an impressive dope because I have this tickling suspicious that I'm the answer. The other answer is that it takes someone just a bit stupider to be with someone so stupid. Either way, I try not to ask anyone why they do anything they do.

Instead of playing catch or something with me in the backyard we didn't have, or taking my mother out to fancy restaurants this town doesn't have, Sean would be sitting there cross-legged in the den unwrapping the cards and stuffing them right into a box, the foil of the packaging glittering around him like fancy garbage. On the off chance there would be a hard, dusty blade of gum included, he'd give it to me if I asked before he stuffed it into his own breathing mouth. Card gum you've got to incubate and soften in the hot wetness of your mouth before you can even threaten to dream of trying to chew it. But in all that time it takes to get soft, you end up realizing you don't want it anyway.

When he took off, like his hero Ben Rooney, Sean had amassed twenty-nine boxes of sports cards. Who knows what he spent. But, unlike Ben Rooney, Sean left all his cards behind when he left. He must have realized what they were really worth. The drool on his pillow on the couch hadn't even dried when Mom packed up those boxes and spirited them to Toronto and to the first comic and sports memorabilia store she found in the phone book.

Rudy—the owner of *Rudy's*, where we took Sean's boxes of currency—had to peel the cards off of each other. Sean must not have even looked at the cards, not caring what they were or what they were about. The cards went from package to box untouched, unenjoyed. Just money in the bank to him. I pretended to browse the stupid store while Mom watched Rudy like a hawk that has no idea what a hawk eats.

Rudy, who was dressed entirely in denim—and I mean entirely: a snap-up denim shirt under a fraying denim jacket covered in buttons of all the major league ball teams, and jeans, and a denim hat from the '88 Calgary Olympics, and even his beard was that yellow colour that jeans become when they rot—Rudy offered us $300 for all twenty-nine boxes. Mom lost it.

She started screaming and all the grown men in the store looked up from the comics they were reading and the action figures they were playing with. How dare Rudy try to take advantage of a destitute and heartbroken widow who was selling her beloved husband's beloved collection to take care of her ailing, beloved son, who had contracted AIDS—that's right! Goddamned, fucking AIDS, Rudy!—from the blood transfusion he needed after the car crash that had killed her beloved husband? "Fuck you, Rudy!" Mom yelled, as if her and Rudy went way, way back, and she stormed out. She sat out in the car and left me, god-damned fucking AIDS and all, to lug the twenty-nine boxes from Rudy's counter back out to the car.

She didn't say it, but I could tell that Mom, in her heart of hearts—yes, the heart that she has inside of her heart—I could tell that in there she actually believed that after one look at all those boxes, Rudy would open his register and count out one million dollars for her, bill by bill. Like Rudy would take the top off the first box, and this golden glow would bathe him like the bath he needed like we needed a million dollars. Rudy? Dressed-all-in-denim Rudy? The heart inside of your heart is full of shit. Ask around.

As he stacked the last few boxes into my arms, Rudy, a bit jittery from having been screamed at, gave me a message to give to my mom. The economy of baseball cards is just like any other economy: it depends on lack. Not many people collected cards in the 50s, say, or their moms threw all the cards into the trash, so cards from then are hard to come by. The harder a card from that time is to come by, the more some guy who's sporting wood for that stuff is willing to cough up for it. When everyone realized how much some people were willing to pay for these useless things, they started holding on to their cards, dreaming of their own million-dollar payoff. But because everyone is collecting now, nothing is rare, and so a collection like Sean's is barely worth the cardboard it's printed on.

I said thanks to Rudy and assured him that I really didn't have AIDS. "Yet," I added, and winked, and the look he gave me said that his friendliness was spent and now it was time to get the fuck out of his store and leave him to surf online undisturbed for that rare pair of denim underwear he needed to complete his set.

I passed Rudy's message on to my mom on the drive home, but telling my mom anything she doesn't want to hear is like trying to give a cat a vitamin. Her fuckbag husband's cards were worth a million dollars and that was all. The next weekend we had a booth at the Big Green Dick Arena, and the new challenge set before me was getting my mom to understand the difference between a booth and a fold-out card table.

From out of twenty-nine boxes and from out of who knows how many cards, the pile, with his baby penis fingers, plucks out just this one card.

"I'll take this," the pile says, and holds up the card like he's a magician who has just found my eight of clubs in the deck.

"Okay," I say, and I fix my stare on his deep snowman eyes, but only because I'm trying to ignore the way that his claw has something like a slimy sheen to it.

"So how much?" the pile says. He makes for his fanny pack, which is a NASA fanny pack.

"I don't know." But I'm not thinking about the card. I'm thinking about an astronaut, done up in all his expensive hubbub, wearing one of those crappy fanny packs.

"I'll tell you what: I'll give you five dollars for it. It's not even worth a buck, frankly, but I don't like breaking bills."

"Let's see it," I say, and take the baseball card from him. It's some guy named Rance Davis, a player for Seattle. His action shot has him in mid-swing. "Who is this guy?"

"He's nobody."

"Nobody's nobody," I say into the pile's eyes, but even against all my best trying, I steal a glance at the claw.

"Davis played like two games in the majors before f'ing his knee for good trying to steal home," the pile says, like this is common knowledge and I'm an idiot for not knowing. "He might have been somebody before, but now he's nobody."

The pile's good hand is out, his baby penises squirming, eager to take the card back. He's getting nervous, you can tell. The pile's starting to quiver like there's something else alive inside of him that's moving around in there, trying to fit in him better.

"If this kid's nobody then why do you want the card?"

"I couldn't give a crap about Davis. He's just the last card I need to finish the '03 Upper Deck season." The pile actually makes a little lunge to reclaim Rance but I rear back. I'm not done with it.

As much as I think professional athletes are overpaid and just plain unnecessary, I can still appreciate that what they do's not easy. A guy doesn't just fall into playing major league baseball. The majors are no chainsaw factory. From when before you can make decisions about what you like or don't, you've got to be irrevocably committed to this stupid, silly lifestyle. I know these majors-bound kids in school, and they're just as weird and destroyed as the military-bound ones. You live your life with blinders on, and you work so foolishly hard against the foolish odds that all that foolish work will just lead up to nothing because hardly any-fucking-body makes it to the major leagues, and even most of the guys who do make it all the way there end up being these anonymous henchman types like this Rance Davis guy the pile is so goddamn engorged for.

I take another look at the card. Maybe the picture is of Rance's first game ever, of his first time at bat. Maybe this is the first pitch, and he's swinging. You give all your dumb life to do this one thing, who are you not to swing? And right as he is here in this picture, there's no telling what will happen. He might swing and miss, or he might scalp that ball. Whatever happens, something will happen. That's what Rance has decided.

T-ball was as far as I played baseball. Hitting a T-ball is just about as easy as punching the air, but there were those kids I remember who just wouldn't or couldn't swing. The ball was elevated and still and unmistakably orange—basically in a choice position for them to be marvelous champions. But so many of those kids would just stand there, bat on their shoulder, not quite ready to swing. Not quite ready for anything to happen because of something they did. Not quite ready for everything to happen because of something they did.

To know that not long after this first swing Rance will screw up his leg and bring to a halt to everything he has been building is just a bit too big. And it's kind of amazing. That all of that is here in this card, this guy's whole life. So I tell the pile it's not for sale.

"Fuck you it's not for sale," the pile yelps. There's just a glimmer of cry in his grown man snowman eyes. "Fuck you it's not for sale!"

A smile comes up like a burp, and I try to allay the thing by wrapping it up, by curling my bottom lip over my top, but the look you make trying to keep yourself from smiling is a million dollars worse than an actual smile. Red flowers bloom all over the pile's pear face until it's just one big field of crimson. Little angry toots of breath fart out of his dilated nostrils and he's wobbling and vibrating just so.

These men that crowd The Arena are basically boys, guarding the crap they have and conniving to steal the crap they want. Action figures and toy cars that they never got to have when they were the right age, memorabilia of athletes that did stuff that these men in a million years would never be able to do, comic books wrapped tight in their Mylar bags, never to be opened again. They bicker and they bitch, all squirrelly greed and mean loneliness. Sometimes I'll watch them milling and waddling around the rink and imagine their bellies as hatches that open up to reveal some petty, pouting child at the controls of a man. The world that these goons live in is so damned fragile, patched together mostly with opinion, so they're so extra careful and possessive of it. The world as they see it is this toy that they won't let anyone else handle because they're afraid it might be taken away from them, or get broken. I haven't heard the phrase "See with your eyes and not with your hands" so often since I can't even remember when.

The pile tries to collect his huffiness, arrange it into something big and threatening. His little claw looks like it's trying to grip air while his other hand keeps adjusting the hang of his shoulder bag. Some sort of panicked dew has settled onto his lip beard, making it glisten.

"I don't know what the hell your deal is, kid. I don't know what kind of shit you're trying to pull, but trust me, I'm not the guy you want to be pulling it with." The pile sputters this out and all I can think of is shit being pulled on one of those machines like taffy.

"I'm not pulling any crap. There's no deal. The card's just not for sale."

"Well why the hell isn't it?"

I take another look at the card, at the mid-swing of Rance Davis, of everything behind him and everything in front of him.

"Because I want it," I tell the pile without looking at him. I don't know how much more I can stand to look at him. "I like this one."

The pile opens his mouth a few times, like he's imitating someone talking. He stops gulping and puts his good hand into one of the boxes and takes out a wad of cards. "Well what about these ones? Huh? You like these ones? Are these ones for sale? Huh?"

"I don't know. I haven't had a look at those ones. Maybe they are."

"Then have a look," the pile says, and he winds up and chucks the wad of cards at me.

For an impossible instant, this wad of maybe a hundred

or so cards about the thickness of a junior hamburger holds its shape in the air, coming at me like one complete block ready to hit my face like I hit it first. But right in front of me each card catches its own influence of air and they pull apart and go their separate ways. All the cards fall, and flutter, and spin, and swoop down, each of them with someone's whole life, some heavy moment, on it.

We stare at each other, the pile and me, like we can't believe that what just happened just happened. As if two other people were doing this, and we were just two guys that watched it. My eyes flit back to the pile's claw and whatever pause button got pushed gets pushed again to make things play. "You're cleaning that up," I say, which I guess presses the pile's own play button, because his mouth opens to say something and his baby penis hand goes to readjust his bag, but before he can say anything, my mom does.

"Pickle!" she yells, and drops to her hands and knees to gather up the scattered cards. There may as well be hundred dollar bills all over the ground. "Fuck, fuck, fuck, fuck," she's mumbling.

What can anybody do but watch something like that? The pile and me set our differences aside like soldiers on Christmas and watch my mom scramble around on the ground. But then I get a glimpse down her shirt and that's enough of that.

"Mom," I say. "Get up. Jesus."

She wobbles onto one knee and reaches to the pile for help up. Her hand grabs at the empty air where a person without a deformed hand's hand would be. She looks up and she sees the claw, in all its shine and sheen, so she gets up just fine on her own. Up, she has that dizzy, frazzled look of someone just spun ceaselessly in a chair.

"So who wants to tell me what the fuck this is?" she says. I can smell on her the cigarettes she doesn't smoke anymore. "Pickle?"

"This is your kid?" the pile wants to know. "These are your cards? This is your table?"

Mom looks at the pile, and then at the mess of cards that she didn't even begin to clean up, and then at the pile's sweaty claw, and then at me, and she seems actually unsure of whether anything here is actually hers. "And you are?" she asks the pile, maybe to bide some time while she figures out who all this stuff belongs to exactly.

"I'm the guy your kid is trying to screw."

"Pickle?"

"I didn't lay a hand on him, Mom, I swear," I say, and though she doesn't, I can tell that my mom wants to smile at that one.

"Listen. Are these cards for sale or aren't they?"

"What? Of course they're for sale."

"Then why won't this kid of yours sell me this card?"

"What card?"

"That one." The pile makes a motion in my direction with his claw, to Rance Davis. "He says it's not for sale because he *likes* it."

I shoot the pile one hell of a look, as if he's betrayed some confidence.

Mom takes the card and I let her take it. She looks it over, stares seriously at it, like someone staring at the engine of a broken down car they have no idea about, as if seriousness will fix the car.

"I don't get it," she says. She turns to me. "What is there to like about it?" Like Sean, she's never taken a look at any of these cards but is so stupidly sure of their worth.

Not knowing what to say, I shrug my shoulders. With my face I do my best to explain about the card, about what's on there to like, but trying to say anything on purpose with your face is like trying to perform a song you hear in your head on an instrument you just barely know how to play.

It goes to show that you never know what anybody is ever thinking. But you can guess, if you know the person. For all I know, my mom isn't thinking about the card right now at all, but about whether or not this pile of human being uses his damp claw to pull his pud. But I don't think she's thinking that. It is probably only me who's thinking that. What I think she's thinking about, seeing the way her face gets full and soft from looking at however my face is looking, has to do with Sean. I bet dimes to dollars that she's suspecting that I don't want to sell the pile this card, or any of these cards, because they're Sean's. Like this is all I've got left of that bag of dicks, and so letting go of his cards would be letting go of him. I think that's the way that someone who watches too much TV's mind tends to work. So she nods at me, having gleaned all she's gleaned from whatever my face had to say. Like, "It's okay. I get it." All I know is that whatever she gets, it can't be it.

My mom turns dramatically to the pile. "I'm sorry," she says, with this weird, fluffy confidence. "The card," she pauses, "is not for sale."

"I'll give you one hundred dollars," the pile says.

"One hundred dollars?" she asks.

"One hundred dollars," the pile confirms.

She can't even afford me a piteous, I'm sorry look. "Okay," my mom says.

Now, anyone that's spent any time being nine years old knows that in any instance of wheeling and dealing you have to see the money before letting someone put their claws on what you're selling. Because even if they do take off without paying you, you at least know that they've got the money to make it worth chasing them down and beating it out of them. Without seeing a nickel, my mom hands over Rance Davis. As soon as the pile has it clutched in his baby penises he brings the card up to his claw, as if to feed an animal he's got in a headlock, and tears the card in half and lets the halves flutter stupidly onto the ground with the rest of the mess he's made so far.

"Fuck you," he says to my mom, pointing an erect baby penis at her.

"Fuck you," he says to me, pegging me with the same baby boner.

"So fuck us both, then?" I ask.

The pile smiles at me, his mustache like an eyebrow over a sick yellow eye. "That's right." We finally understand each other.

Giving his shoulder bag one final, absolute adjustment, the pile galumphs away.

All the other men in all their other fanny packs are staring at us. I'm looking at my mom, trying to decide whether or not I can hate her for the rest of my life because of this, if this one time is enough of a reason. Every last Sunday I come here with her, for her—not that I have anything better to do—and entertain this insane delusion of hers. All this for her, and she's ready to sell me out in an instant. People have hated people for less.

I guess because someone has to say something, my mom turns to me and, instead of "I'm sorry," she makes a gross face and says, "Did you get a load of that asshole's little hand?"

"Yeah," I agree. "It was disgusting."

Like we'd rehearsed it before, we both, at the exact same time, screw up our faces and distort our left hands and make this guttural noise—like, "Grarrrrrrrrr"—and this is going to go on to be a shared thing that we do whenever something's disgusting or unreasonable in life. We make the hand, do the noise, and know exactly where all that came from.

# THE SHREW'S DILEMMA

For something like five years now the man who was what amounts to this woman's first love has been dead, and she's only finding out now. To alert her, there was no shiver along an ethereal web of life connecting everyone, as there maybe should have been, or as this woman at least hoped there would be when something like this happens. Her heart didn't even murmur in sympathy the moment her one-time heartthrob's own heart quit its throbbing. This woman's sister had to tell her, mention it—his passing—in passing.

"There's something with you," says this woman's boyfriend that night.

"Jonathan Brandis is dead," she admits. "He hung himself."

"Hanged," her boyfriend whispers, then fits his hand back between this woman's thighs, his hot, wet face back into her neck.

The day after she finds out about Jonathan Brandis, this woman's subway is delayed. An expensive-looking woman on the platform beside her explains that someone has jumped. "Don't worry," the expensive woman says, trying to be nice. "It happens so much that they can clean the mess up like that." And she snaps her fingers.

This woman is late for her interview at the gallery. A reception job for the summer. "I'm so sorry," she says, rushing finally to the reception desk. "My train was delayed."

The current receptionist looks up from a crossword puzzle, a woman this woman remembers meeting through her boyfriend. "The buses, too?" the receptionist asks, not recognizing this woman. Her head is shaved bald and she has a spider web tattoo there where her hair would be and she is not sympathetic in the least. "And the taxis?"

The receptionist has filled in only one clue of the puzzle, this woman can see. "Torpor."

This woman doesn't get the job. Not because she was late, necessarily. She blames her unsuitable phone voice. Callers never know whether they're speaking with a fancy-ish man or a gravelly woman, and they get uncomfortable. Her boyfriend uses words like throaty, and smoky, and loves the daylights out of it.

She takes the streetcar to her apartment and showers without getting her hair wet. Smoking the shake of her stash mixed with tobacco, she watches the news for some mention of the man who jumped. On the news there is nothing but death reported, just not this one death. Maybe there wasn't any man after all. Except that expensive woman had seemed so sure.

Come sunset, her boyfriend arrives with sushi and beer. In their circle this woman calls him either her lover or her partner, or simply by name, but she still can think of him only as her boyfriend. Those other terms sound too pretentious to her. They suggest a level of intention and participation that this woman is not yet willing to consider, or at least not yet willing to admit.

Always she wakes up before him. She waits around in bed for him to rouse is the sort of woman this woman is. She will read a book or sketch or just lie there. This morning she watches her boyfriend sleep. This is the first man she has seriously shared a bed with ever. At the start she watched him as a kid will incessantly inspect the first dollar they've earned for themselves, and a little of that disbelief and fascination still lingers. He looks to her like he sleeps as if he knows he's being watched is how perfectly and quietly he sleeps.

She checks in on his penis. Mostly the thing will be as asleep as its owner, but this morning it's awake and beating. This woman conducts a test. She puts her ear to her boyfriend's chest with the attention of a safe cracker but can't discern a delay between when his heart thubs and when his wiener throbs. That's how fast his blood must travel.

This peeking is weird, but she knows he wouldn't have a problem if he found out. This woman wonders about how into it he'd be. Worries as much as wonders.

With no job for the summer yet, this woman's hands are a mess with time. Though her parents are covering her costs during the school year, they refuse to support her during the summer. Her options were to either get a job in the city or come back home, move back into her high school bedroom for a few months. Part of her trusts, though, that the support won't be cut off.

June days in the city are heavy as a wet sweater, and leaving her apartment with no clear purpose has lately required unprecedented gumption on her part. After JB and after this man on the subway she didn't know from Adam—if there even was a man—this woman spends her mornings trolling the obits for announcements where the cause of death isn't mentioned. There are scores of them, and she imagines every single one is a suicide. Like when she found all those maggots in the apartment. The act of discovering the first one seemed to spawn a crawling, writhing heap of others. And now, all of a sudden, the world is full of people killing themselves.

Instead of working on her painting or looking for work, this woman reads on the computer about dolphins in captivity who dash their brains to mush against the walls of their tank. It goes that a dolphin named Kathy swam up to her trainer one day, looked at him in a meaningful way, and then dove back down for good. Dolphins lack the involuntary breathing reflex that humans have, that matter-over-mind pull that would have forced a man to surface in this case. Kathy the dolphin stayed at the bottom of her container and died without a fuss or shiver.

JB worked with a dolphin on SeaQuest. Could there be a connection?

This woman feels like she could cry, but doesn't make it there.

She watches him in rented movies. *Ladybugs*, *Sidekicks*, *The Neverending Story II*. They aren't as good as she remembers them. In *Sidekicks*, JB overcomes his asthma through martial arts. How is this possible? Even under the redheaded tutelage of Chuck Norris.

Pausing the movie, squatting before the TV, she searches his angular, adorable face for some explanation. This woman can't get over how girly JB was, how beautiful. His dirty blonde hair, his popsicle-stained lips, a blush to his cheeks like he has just come in from the cold. This isn't attraction, only the memory of attraction, which, in itself, is stirring.

As she did not that long ago with pictures torn carefully from her teenybopper magazines, this woman plants one on the frozen frame.

How bad could things have gotten?

In the dust on the screen, the blotch of her smooch is not at all in the shape of her lips.

On the internet she finds a quote from Schopenhauer. "It will generally be found," he said, "that where the terrors of life come to outweigh the terrors of death a man will put an end to his life."

"You have a fine body," he says over breakfast. All morning her boyfriend has been goading her into being naked with him. The muggy day is on his side. "What's the big stink?"

On most Sundays, when he stays for the morning, he won't dress at all. Naked when he makes breakfast, naked when he reads The Star on the couch, naked when he does the dishes. She wears underwear to weigh herself even is the sort of woman this woman is.

She has seen old pictures and for his whole life he has been attractive, whereas her features are something she had to grow into, make the best of, and will eventually grow out of. That airy gap between her front teeth, that pike of a neck, those lucent eyebrows, those papercut lips. Bangs were a revelation, curtains she could draw over a pimpled forehead that some girls in her high school had called an eighthead. But in bed with him, when he's astride her, those bangs can't help but fall to the side, which wouldn't be a problem if he didn't always have his eyes wide open as he fucks her. In a perfect world, she would be on top and her hair would cover her face, except this woman has trouble moving up there, can only really shift around like in an uncomfortable easy chair, and also hates the way her breasts dangle and the way her stomach bunches. In a perfect world he would be blindfolded, or they would do it with a sheet between them, or she would just feel good about herself. In a perfect world JB would not be dead.

"You have it better than most people," she says.

"Better how?" Wet cereal falls from his mouth and into his naked lap, and even this doesn't strike her as at all slovenly.

"You've never been ugly," she says.

"That's not fair to say."

Months ago—nearly seven of them—he approached her as if she was put there for him to take is how they got together. It matters very much that he chose her at his vernissage, that his work was what was being held up to where the light could get at it that night. She still hasn't asked him about the women in the show's paintings, their bared bodies all perfect in their specificity, or at least perfect in his renderings. She worries about being seen as a worrier. One body was hulkingly obese, another delicately emaciated, the next scarred by an appendectomy, still another so pregnant that the belly hung over her crotch so that it appeared to have an evil goatee. Whoever those women were, or had been, it was only their bodies, after all. Her boyfriend had replaced their heads with a cat head, an elephant head, a chimp head, a dolphin head, to roaring success. All the women at the show agreed.

It matters very much that he was being followed that night by all the other young first-year, moody-looking artist girls, with their bangs like hers, and their glasses like hers, and their layers of sweaters like hers, who were saying *vernissage* for the first time in their lives too, and who had also helped themselves to a few too many second glasses of the complimentary wine. It matters a stinking ass-load that he had and will always have seven years on her. It matters that he is muscular without having to try, and that his teeth were never askew enough to need braces, and that he had a fading black eye at the time. And though things are going well enough between them now, this woman can't forget that she began—looking back—in such a detestable position of flighty girlyness. All of this matters more than she wants it to.

"Why are you on about this anyway? What's it to you if I'm nude or not?"

"Because being the only one naked feels silly."

"Then put some pants on for fucks sake."

"The Shrew's Dilemma" is what this one's called. This woman's boyfriend warns her about naming a painting before she's finished, let alone even begun. But it's basically all done in her head. She sees a series. Big canvases, loads of blood. This woman has never painted blood before, and can't wait. All the reds, browns and purples to mix: rufous, sangria, rust, sinopia, Tyrian—maybe even a squidge of her own life stuff in there. She thinks that from now on gore might be her thing.

The story goes that three shrews are placed under an overturned tumbler. Shrews have a metabolism that leaves them always needing to eat, so the shrew lives his entire life in search of food, making him—regardless and in spite of his size—one of the most terrible predators when you're talking mammals. And somehow three of these guys get trapped beneath a tumbler. Two of them waste no time eating up the third. A few hours pass and, without batting a beady eye, the hungrier of the remaining two turns on his friend. This final captive is observed proudly cleaning his whiskers afterwards is how few scruples he has with cannibalism. In no time the last man standing is hungry again and gets an eyeful of his own tail. Starting there, the shrew is supposed to eat himself to death.

"What do you think?" she asks him. This morning she is trying to make the three shrews trapped beneath the tumbler adorable enough without anthropomorphizing them, but still can't quite.

He is sitting in just his underwear on the windowsill, his legs dangling out, clipping his toenails into the alley below. "Well, what are you trying to say with it?"

"I guess it's a comment about life," she says.

"What about life?"

"I don't know."

"Well," says her boyfriend, swinging around to straddle the sill. "There's your problem."

"So Jonathan Brandis is dead," this woman tells a friend over lunch, a girlfriend, who laughs. This girlfriend has a government grant to make a short film that Rick Moranis has apparently expressed interest in coming out of retirement to do and so is paying for the meal. "He hanged himself."

"You mean the teenybopper guy? Are you serious? I used to love that guy. That's hilarious."

When she was tacking pictures of Jonathan Brandis to her walls her older sister was pinning up Kurt Cobain. Cobain seemed then to this woman an older, uglier, more morose version of Jonathan Brandis. When Cobain opened the back of his skull with a shotgun, her sister carved *Kurt* into her own arm. She laughs about it now, this woman's sister does, how dramatic she had been, but there must have been some legitimate wound left, even if it was misguided or put on. In as much as she was capable of love at that age, she loved Kurt Cobain. When her sister laughs she must be laughing at herself, like when this woman sees a photo from when she was ten, wearing a pink tracksuit that she loved, and can't help but titter, nervously.

"Why's that hilarious?" this woman hazards to ask her friend. Like her boyfriend, this friend is a few years older than her. This woman fell in with this older community all on account of him. Months now, and she has not exactly gotten over the certainty that they make fun of her behind her back and that a split with her boyfriend will mean a split from everyone.

"It's hilarious because it's Jonathan Brandis, I guess."

"But you loved him."

"Maybe not like you did."

"You said 'love.'"

"Puppy love."

This woman chews on it, watches a soiled man with a green beard stagger past the window, his eyes wide and amazed. She hasn't been in the city long enough to look past the homeless. She has no urge to help, just can't help but ogle them.

"And the way you love now is different," she comes around to say.

"I've grown up," the friend says.

"And you'll keep on doing that."

"Like how?"

"Like laughing at the way you were kind of says that you're, you know, above that now, right?"

Her friend tucks a curl of hair behind her ear and picks at her plate. "Fine."

"So someday you'll move on to laugh at everything that means the world to you at this instant. Everything you love."

"This Jonathan Brandis killing himself thing really got to you, huh?"

"You know my father committed suicide," this woman says.

Cheek puffed out with empanada, her friend pauses, this hollow look of horror in her eyes.

"Jesus," she says, the wet mess of her meal gawking out of her mouth. "Fuck. I'm sorry, Emma. I didn't know."

Of course this woman's father never killed himself and she suspects that this friend of hers was the one with the cat head, the one with the appendectomy scar, the painting fawned over by every viewer the night of his show. The number her boyfriend will sometimes call from her place.

"Help me help you," she whispers in the dark, attempting to somehow sound sexy in this desperate position, holding him uncertainly, with a mannequin's grip.

"Don't worry about me," he says, reaching again between her legs as if for a bowling ball. "Getting you off gets me off."

Maybe her boyfriend is a little too good at all this sex stuff. He flips over her cover page with the aplomb of a student who can't wait to ace a test, whereas this woman hasn't got a clue what she's doing, stares dreadfully at the questions put before her.

Working away at her, he moans more than she does, is more out of breath than this woman is after she has come. Though his is a different sort of pleasure, she is sure.

She wakes up later that night having to piss. Already

his rambunctiousness has given her two urinary tract infections. His side of thc bed is empty and the ensuite bathroom glows at its cracks. With an ear to the door this woman hears the sound of one hand clapping. She climbs back into bed, still having to pee.

Having sex with JB never crossed her mind. As a girl, she dreamt of going to dinner and a movie with him, of having her mom drive her to the mall and drop her off there, where she would meet with JB by the fountain. And then marriage, eventually. There wasn't one salty drop of prurience to that attraction. This woman never thought about having JB sweat on her, or having him scrape her calf with a toenail, or having him wake her up in the mornings with a harmless erection jabbing her in the hip. She never imagined having conversations with JB. What would they have talked about? JB had been no different than a baby doll that wets itself, something girls coddle and care for to prepare themselves for the real thing. He had been a tool, an aid: light, stiff, plastic and unkillable.

When her boyfriend returns to bed, she rolls into him, thinking to broach the problem, only he reads this as her asking, and so graciously lays once more into her. Lord only knows how many minutes later, this woman is exhausted, doesn't know what's what and has to pee worse than before.

"Thanks," she exhales, dumbly combing her hair back over her forehead.

With her windows closed, the rain outside is only the crinkling and snapping sounds of a campfire left to burn itself out. In the crotchy heat of her apartment this woman removes everything but a light dress shirt he has left there, which smells of cigarettes, and sweat, and boy. She stretches out on her couch and looks at "The Shrew's Dilemma" across the room from her, still unfinished after a month. With one eye closed, she gropes for it with her toes. Tonight is too hot for anything. All July has been too hot for jack fucking shit.

When she was a girl, this woman was taught to treat life like a gift, and she has done her best. For others, though, this gift must be no better than a gaudy sweater too long in the arms, knit for them by some doddering relative they can't recall ever actually meeting. Some will wear that gift dutifully, with the fear that that old relative will stop by unannounced one of these days. They don't want to be rude, so they feign appreciation always, in case. The others—those that dump themselves in front of subway trains, those that loop nylon rope around their necks—they return that gift to the sender, with a note that says, You don't know me at all.

Only JB didn't leave a note. This woman read on the internet that he didn't.

A few times she phones her boyfriend and every time hangs up before the machine. His message always tricks her in to thinking he has picked up and said Hello, and every time she feels stupid, like he's making fun of her.

You can't help but imagine life before you live it, she thinks. For her first two decades she played out the rest of her life in her head. How she would move to the city, study art, make enough money making sandwiches in a collectively owned vegan café to rent a loft but not enough to fully furnish or heat it, be thought of as a marvelous painter for her age, become strong and independent so as to survive turbulent, passionate relationships with brilliant and troubled men who grow full beards and write poetry as sarcastic as it is beautiful. Why else would you strike out into the world if you hadn't first considered what you might find out there, and how amazing all of it would be? No one is born stupid enough to knowingly enter a hard and hurtful fate. You have to trick yourself into getting out and into it, or be tricked.

The days following his opening this woman imagined the two of them staying inside for entire weekends, painting, being so involved in the work that neither would notice when one side of a mixtape ran out, passing by each other's work spaces sometimes and smiling. There would be parties at his place on weeknights, with red wine and organic food, and someone's homemade ice cream. Parties that weren't planned but that happened as each person stopped by unannounced, until his kitchen, living room and balcony became a tumult of opinions, one overlapping over the other: highfalutin, overly intellectual, but still informed by a very honest and relevant curiosity. They would plan sex, but become busy with other things, fucking instead in unexpected bursts and unexpected places. Maybe some public hand jobs. They would cut each other's hair. They would expect nothing of each other and get everything

Since the winter he hasn't worked on anything that she knows about. He eats fast food without apology and never invites her over, preferring instead to show up unannounced at her place, which, hardly a loft, is beginning to feel more tank-like the less she goes out. Sex is a given and expected. And she is smarter than him. He once insisted that Charles Dickens was the author of *Don Quixote*. Sunday afternoons he disappears and she only just found out that he is classically trained on the guitar.

She calls her friend—the one from the café—who does not pick up and who does not have a machine. Maybe she is meeting with Rick Moranis. Maybe she's fucking Rick Moranis.

You can only ever have an idea of another person, a sort of surrogate you create in your imagination, or your heart, or whatever stupid place. Feelings of betrayal come when that person wanders outside the parameters you gave them. This woman admits to herself that she can never know her boyfriend, but only harbor an idea of him. To be with anyone for a stretch of time, to do anything for any significant duration, to live happily, demands a readiness for surprises and constant, willing revision.

Life is not hard, she thinks, staring across the room at "The Shrew's Dilemma," straining her toes to touch it, life is only life. Hardships are bred by our expectations.

"Hardships are bred by our expectations," this woman says out loud. So what is suicide, then, but the consequence of a broken-down imagination? An inability to put a happy, hopeful face on any and all situations.

This woman wonders what it was JB wanted so badly that he would kill himself in its absence. Her problem is that she can only imagine JB as giving, and can't even begin to conceive his wants. As a girl, she took for granted that he would be interested in her. She wanted him, really, only because he was dreamy. Her pimpled eighthead, her shyness, the speech impediment from her retainer, all this would not factor in his love for her. He would just love her.

Her initial shock didn't come from finding out that Jonathan Brandis was dead, but from finding out that he had been alive, that he had continued to exist long after she lost interest in him.

Unable to stand the heat any longer, this woman gets up off the couch and opens the window. The sweaty air in her apartment rushes past her, is sucked out into the cooling night, lifting up the tails of his shirt, giving the city an eyeful. The rush slams her bedroom door behind it like a teenager throwing a tantrum and nearly sucks "The Shrew's Dilemma," in progress, from its easel.

A bird flies into the window this morning while they are fucking, just as the tendrils of orgasm are beginning to curl up her spine. This woman will not say *make love*. She finds the phrase misleading, like fast food *restaurant*: a stab at glamourizing and romanticizing something so sloppy and inexpensive.

The bird collapses the house of cards she has built and nabs the concentration needed to build it back up again, so this woman makes a loud, writhing show of getting off, for his sake. In the residue left by rain and dust on the window is the imprint of the bird, which looks nothing like a bird.

This woman has read on the internet about oxytocin. She knows enough to know that she is biologically predisposed to fall in love with whoever makes her come. It's the same hormone she will release if she ever gives birth, is what will supposedly endear that child to her for the rest of her and its life. Maybe in this way only is *making love* a workable term. Except now, having skipped that release, this woman is not so fooled. She is not blurry like usual and sees the smug smile of satisfaction on his face.

"How long should fruit be kept out on the counter?" she asks. "Should it be pitched before or after it has gone rotten? Because by the time the signs of decomposition start to show it's already too late, right?"

"Stop that," he says. "Don't be weird."

From here on in, she knows, their relationship will only get worse, until the time comes when the pain of being together becomes greater than the pain of being apart. It's childish, this woman thinks, to think that anything will last forever, but it is craven, she knows, to avoid something only because it will end. What he thinks, about this or anything, she can't say. He's just lying there, smiling.

"What's the problem?" he asks. "I think it works."

"It's not really what I was aiming for."

The problem is that the shrew is a hideous little thing after all. There was not a human enough face she could fit on it. Its scraggly dun fur, its wrinkled, pointy snout, its eyes too beady to contain even a pinch of thought or emotion. A beast doing a beastly thing is not as meaningful as this woman hoped it would be. For the shrew there is no pickle. He gets peckish, he eats.

The problem, she realized finally, lay in the shrew's captivity. A desperate enough shrew will hold its breath under water to kill a fish over twice its own size by nibbling out its eyes and finally its brain. This is comparable to a regular-sized man battling an elephant with a plastic bag over his head. This is all on the internet. Working against the shrew is what a dolphin lacks, that invisible grip on its scruff that will yank it to the surface regardless of desperation. Maybe there is no apparent danger when there is another shrew to eat, but left finally alone, that last shrew would make some attempt to free itself before resorting to its last resort.

This woman's solution was to add, to that last bloody painting, a dainty index finger holding the cup in place. A finger from a graceful, fluid hand—not dissimilar from the finger of Michelangelo's God that sparked life and thought into his reaching Adam. Only, added weeks after she thought she finished the painting, the finger stands out as what it is: an afterthought.

No painting of hers ever seems to come out the way she intendeds. Realizing this and not knowing how to turn back, completing the thing becomes a cinch. With no real investment she can give the painting what it needs instead of hopelessly trying to force onto it what she wants.

"Who cares what you think?" her boyfriend says. At least he's dressed.

"How bad would your life have to get for you to kill yourself?" she asks later that night.

The question comes in the soggy silence following almost two hours between the sheets. Through perseverance and jelly, she was finally able to finish him off.

"What?" He's genuinely winded and she's glad for that.

"Under what circumstances would you, you know, end it?"

"I don't know," he sighs. "Don't be weird, Emma."

"Say you were paralyzed from the neck down, or say you had your arms and legs blown off and couldn't talk and were stuck inside your own thoughts, like in that Metallica video. Or everyone you cared about abandoned you and you were left with absolutely nothing in your life."

"Do we have to talk about this?"

"We do."

"Then my answer is I would never kill myself. Simple as that. Suicide is the most selfish thing a person can do."

"Okay," she says, and nuzzles her head back onto his shoulder, spreading her hand on his chest. Past the bracken of his chest hair, past his skin, past his meat and past his ribs, there is the faint flutter of his settling heart, his beating heart, something she can only feel if she is quiet enough, and patient enough, and knows what she's looking for, something that, when finally found, she can easily verify by that same obvious cadence she sees in his fading erection.

And what is love, really, this woman thinks to herself, if not selfish?

# UNBURDENED THINGS

I don't think I want to be the kind of person anymore that brings tears to things unnecessarily.

Like, say, "Belly's missed us," I'll say when our cat returns from a week off exploring, hunting mice, probably, in the few condemned factories in the neighborhood that haven't been turned into condos yet. "Look," I'll show my boyfriend, "She's crying."

Cradling her, making a slim ghost of his finger with a tissue, Kim will wipe away the line of goo in the corner of Belly's eye. "The Bully's been fighting is all," he'll say. Belly will not allow herself to be held by me, will writhe and twist until she either falls or I drop her. "Bullies never cry."

Or else, we're under the trees after a summer rain, say. Kim and I will be on a stroll and a breeze will ruffle the leaves, and we get sprinkled. Like the tree's sobbing all over us.

I can bring tears to pretty much anything without having to try.

And I gather from this that I'm either overly emotional or underly creative, and I'd really rather not be any of those ways.

Because it's not that those things don't cry; it's that they can't.

And it's not our business to burden unburdened things with ours.

So:

Kim comes in from the courtyard with drops of water hanging from his earlobes in no way like teardrops. Maybe more like earrings.

They'd ambushed him.

A rush of water balloons and those pump action deals that can soak you from fifty metres away while he was having a beer on our steps after work.

Kim turned the garden hose on them and wrestled their guns away. Turned the tables on those kids.

"We're going to get a phone call," he says, walking into the kitchen, struggling to peel his sopping shirt off his skin. His shorts come off and he's down on the kitchen tile, which is the coolest part of the house during early August. A secret he learned from Belly.

The tongues of his steel-toed boots droop out like the tongues of exhausted dogs in this heat.

When he fights with the neighborhood kids, Kim loses with a stink. They clobber Kim like clockwork and he's such a sore loser. On purpose, though.

Because for a kid nothing's more insulting than having an adult let you beat them. There's no joy of triumph. Only that weird feeling of being patronized. Like the feeling of wearing a shirt backwards. Upon losing, Kim throws a tizzy and won't talk to them for days.

The following afternoon, the kids show up hugging basketballs to their chests and balancing ball bats in their palms.

"What's Kim doing?" they ask.

"Don't tell him I told you," I'll say, "But he's upstairs. Crying. Can't you people take it a little easy on him?"

And they scatter away, triumphant, miffed and still needing a third for Suicide Squeeze.

Of course Kim is really at work, building cookie cutter houses on the crusts of town. These kids think that because they're off of school he gets a break, too.

But I'm afraid if I called them on their oversight, accused them of not knowing how the world really works, probably they'd ask, Well, then what are *you* doing home?

Days later, those people will be on the court behind our house and see us on the roof killing a bowl at dusk.

"Kim, come play!" they call.

They don't even know my name.

Kim's over the fence. He takes the lead, but then falls back by a few points. And that's when he becomes a flurry of elbows, inevitably opening up a young chin under the boards. Kim runs home and hides, leaving me, high as a spooked cat in a tree, to assuage the inevitable moms that will come knocking.

Kim has no problem being fucked up around children. But I can't abide that. If I had a child I would never let it see me drink or drug. Never let it see me cry. Never let it see me rolling pennies at the kitchen table. If it saw me doing any one of those things and asked, Why do you do that? there's no way I could tell it the truth.

Because it's hard sometimes.

Belly flits in through the kitchen window now, sniffs at Kim's sock balls on the floor. She curls up on his bare stomach.

There's a knock at the door.

Kim, lethargic like he just woke up, is running his finger over the grey down on Belly's nubs. She lost most of her ears to frostbite before she was our cat, back when she was someone else's kitten.

Another knock.

Belly will only let you play with her ears until she feels she's being made fun of. She'll try and twitch her ears away from you, only they're too stubby for this to be actually evasive. A bellicose growl and a chomp at your finger if you don't lay off.

A rapping now.

Something I've noticed about cats: this threshold they've got. Comfort is their primary aim. When they've established a cozy place, they grab on firmly with both paws. Like Belly has this way of stretching out across our bed at night so that there is no way for Kim and I to sleep comfortably.

We skitter our hands around her like chaseable critters, trying to tempt her appetite for the hunt.

We tug the blankets.

Mumble, mumble, she goes, ticked but immovable.

Bark, bark, we try, tired and desperate and getting weird.

Jumping up and down on our bed like it was a motel bed is what it takes to get to sleep most nights.

Pounding.

Kim stays put, but Belly looks over at me. She says, Are you going to get that or *what?* Keeping in mind that cats can't talk like they can't cry.

I do.

Three of them, arms raised, gripping swollen, sweating balloons.

The phone rings. I bet you some irate mother.

The kids see that I'm not Kim and they lower their arms. Then off they scamper.

Two separate from the third and unload on him. He

stands betrayed for the length of a commercial before charging after his best friends in the world.

The phone rings and I actually can't remember what it was exactly I was doing before Kim came in.

Are you going to get that or *what?* Belly asks. In her own way.

Once you could bike out to the limits of town to gander at the mostly unbridled night. The Milky Way was a drool stain on a cerulean pillow cover. Now stadium lights illuminate broad burrows and suggestive frames. A shopping centre with a library inside is being raised in anticipation of this burgeoning community.

Life is becoming so crowded and bright these days.

Kim was due there for five. He set the alarm for three.

Why does Kim get up so early?

"Because rolling out of bed and onto the job blows," he says. "I need some allusion of having a life outside of work."

Kim hides the alarm on the other side of the bedroom every night so he has to bound out of bed and scrounge around the laundry like a narcotics dog to silence it every morning. After that panic he's wide awake. And you better believe me too.

Kim always confuses illusion with allusion. And for Kim the Pacific Ocean is Specific also.

For summer coffee we fill the ice cube tray with cream and leave it in the freezer overnight. My idea.

I'm brilliant.

Staring at the ceiling fan over our bed, trying to plan my day, I give Kim a head start.

Kneading the night kinks out of his neck, he's hunched over his sketchbook at the kitchen table. On the counter he's set out my mug for me, unfilled.

Our stove clock wasn't changed when last we leapt ahead. Instead of adjusting it, we learned to read the time wrong. When we fall back we'll have to get used to not correcting ourselves.

Kim squints at the page, trying to see a clear image through the bramble of other ideas. Already he's begun sketches for the graphic novel he will make. He'll be ready to throw himself fully into the project by the time it's my turn to start working.

A few incorrect minutes happen.

I slurp my coffee, reminding him I'm here, too.

"So," he asks perfunctorily. "What're your plans for the day?" Patronizingly.

Kim will never tell me that he hates that I get up with him. Hates that because he's working for me right now he has hardly a moment to himself. And the time he does have, I occupy.

He never says anything like Belly never says anything.

"The Bully's at the window," he says.

I look behind me and, with the kitchen lights on inside, only see me in the pane.

We cut this deal like mustard, Kim and I: for one year he works while I do whatever my heart desires. Then we turn the tables.

Jump back. Fall ahead.

Inside of me I eventually see Belly on the ledge, pawing, going *tack tack tack* on the window. Like a teacher tapping chalk to the right of an equal sign, pleading and impatient.

Like, Come on, kids. You *know* this one.

What I would say if Kim ever said boo, is that it's difficult for me also. It wasn't supposed to be difficult, this year was supposed to be a productive breeze, but there you go. His free time is the only time I have to be with him, otherwise I'm alone. He has too little time and I have too much.

Run a tap hot on your hand and it will become freezing to you in time.

I open up the back door and cluck for Belly to come. She stops pawing and looks at me. Her eyes flare spooky green. She turns back to the window and asks again.

"Belly," I say. "Come on." But she keeps at the window, so I open it. She falls inside and saunters towards her food bowl. I close the door and leave the window open for her to go back out.

I will sit with Kim, not bothering him, until it's time. He will kiss me and split. I will go back to bed and sleep until ten-ish. I will wake back up and have no idea how to get out of bed. I will think about how late in the day it is already, and that to start anything now is pointless because anyway I have to make lunch first. And maybe afterwards I will have to run out to the store for toilet paper, for anything. By the time I get home it will be time for the Sassy Judge Show that I like. It is the gift I give myself for all the hard work I do in a day. After which Kim will be home in an hour from his job. I will make him supper because he works so hard.

A year, and what?

I am no better at the drums, though I can twirl my sticks in a way that would make the ladies in the front row wet, the men hard.

Mr. Dumbface, my dummy, can't talk without me gritting my teeth in a horrible, threatening way that would scare the children at the birthdays I was hoping to perform at.

There isn't a play in my head that doesn't take place at a bus stop or a TV pilot that doesn't take place in a living room.

The pair of socks I'm knitting stay heelless.

A year, and that. And my time's running out, the breadth given to my heart's desire shrinking.

Full, Belly plods to the door and rises up on her hind legs to ask.

"Belly!" I scold. When she sits back down and looks at me I point at the open window. She looks at it, then back to the door. And then me.

Belly always looks at me like she has no idea what I'm talking about.

Kim has gone.

What's that joke about the broken clock again?

The stream of eye goo runnelling along Belly's nose catches the kitchen light and shimmers like a knife come out of nowhere in a fight you didn't think was that serious.

Kim warns me not to give too much of a character to Belly. Like he tells me that trees don't and can't cry. Animals don't think anything, he explains. They don't mean anything. Or at least, they don't think or mean anything that we can understand.

It goes even a broken clock is right two times a day.

There's this rap.

Behind my kit, I'm holding my sticks like a fork and knife, waiting for a late meal to be served finally. Even though lunch has just been smoked.

No dishes.

I'm brilliant.

Three of them. One has a black eye. The other has a scab shaped like an overfed lightning bolt on his shin. The third has corn rows and a basketball at his hip.

All four of us are roughly the same height and have

roughly the same mix of masculinity and femininity to our features but only three of us are rough.

"Kim home?" they want to know.

"I'll play if you want."

Sour, their pusses.

"Two on two," I offer.

"You any good?" the shiner-one asks.

"Good?" I say. "Are you kidding? They don't call me the White Larry Bird for nothing."

So me and Corn Rows versus Shiner and Scabby then.

My signature move is sending the ball into orbit around my waist. They see this and are impressed.

"Kiss your moms at the bus stop," I say, "Because I'm taking you kids to school."

With that, they are further wowed.

Until I check the ball out from my chest like I'm shoving someone. Their eyes roll like shoes in laundromat dryers.

Dribbling up court, Shiner slaps the ball away from me and lays up the first point.

Corn Rows looks at me like, Come on!

This time he checks and Scabby's on him as soon as he passes half court.

I am the wide open Specific Ocean.

I'm unguarded under the net and flagging Corn Rows down like my car has crapped out on the side of the highway. But he makes a break for the hoop anyway. And is denied.

"I was open," I say.

"Didn't see you," he says.

So: two to fuck you.

I check and charge towards half court, jump, plant my feet, and take my shot.

Nothing but air.

There are other things I could be doing right now. Learning Wipe Out, or perfecting that Hole in the Bucket routine with Mr. Dumbface.

Their bodies change after my Hail Mary. Before, they were on the balls of their feet, but now they're flatfooted as detectives. The boys turn languid and gentle.

Carrying the ball, forgetting to dribble, I slip past Shiner and sink my first.

Kim is a stickler, will call all transgressions. A kid looks at him the wrong way and it's a foul. Kim will slap his wrist like he's demanding the proper time. For a travel he will spin his fists, one around the other, in some furious rumba.

"Wasn't that travelling?" I ask.

They exchange glances.

Kim will take his penalty shot and always just barely miss.

"Two-one," they say.

Because I am fifteen years older than them, and obviously a worse basketball player, they let me drive the lane and tie.

They're making allowances now.

Corn Rows is open under the net and I'm being half-heartedly swarmed by Shiner and Scabby. If I'm as bad at basketball as I know I am, then this is all an accident.

If anything, I should be paying *their* allowances.

I feed Corn Rows the rock.

Feed it to him when he isn't looking.

No dishes.

They wanted to end this. So I end it.

In no way like tears, blood dribbles out of Corn Rows' nose and dots his jersey that's as long as a dress.

Then the tear-tears come.

Let them clot their own selves.

At home I hide behind my kit. And the phone bringles.

My first impulse is to start banging away at the skins so as to justify not hearing it. But before I can Belly leaps up—*thump, thump*—and curls up for a nap on my floor tom.

Kim and I went for a walk when I got home from work. It's winter now, somehow.

Belly's been gone two weeks and in that time they've demolished and excavated one of the old factories to make way for condos by the spring. Which means that if Kim were still working he'd only have to travel a block over for work. Kim tells me he looks for Belly in the day, but who knows. He doesn't seem that concerned.

"I've put a missing cat into the book," he says, as if that's something.

Either he doesn't care or he trusts that everything will be okay. Search me for the difference.

Dusk was frigid and quiet and my eyes started to water.

"Everything okay?" Kim asks.

"I'm just getting used to it," I say.

# THE PRICE YOU PAY FOR LEAVING THE HOUSE

I'd been sitting Ames's house a week when a woman came to the door. She sucked apologetically through her teeth when she saw my swim trunks. "You're on your way out," she informed me.

"Just getting back," I lied. "Actually."

She had grown up in the house and wondered if she might look around. Sure, I told her and stepped out of the way for her to come in.

Black Santa's tail puffed and she ran at the sight of the woman, her pink bum stink-eyeing us. This was Black Santa's house before it was mine, and who was this new person all of a sudden?

The woman was attractive in a mature, tired-looking way, the way women are attractive on the bus after everyone's had an ungovernable day. You wonder what they're coming from and where they're headed to, and whether or not you're better than either points. Her hair was curly and simple brown, and short like it had been long and just cut. Her sundress was peach and flimsy, and the tank top she was wearing underneath had some words on it, one of which looked like it might be *KILL*.

"Should I take my shoes off?" she asked, and lifted a foot for demonstration, though she was wearing complicatedly-strapped sandals, not shoes. I looked down at her feet and told her I didn't know.

"There'd been carpet when I was here. Ugly green shag shit. And there was this rule about no shoes on the carpet. The thing was my mom—oh my god, that woman—my mom was disgusted by the sight of people's feet. I mean, like, revolted. *They're like smelly hands gone horribly wrong,* she'd say. Of course in the summer my friends didn't wear socks, so right beside the door here was this wicker basket full of sock balls and if you were in bare feet you had to don a pair."

The woman had actually said don. This was a woman I could love.

"But that carpet was ugly-ass. Of course you got rid of it. I'm glad you got rid of it. What kind of person would have kept it?"

"I didn't," I told her, and she looked at the floor where there wasn't carpet, and then looked at me again. "I mean this isn't my house," I said. "I mean I'm housesitting for the people whose house this is who are on their honey-moon." I rolled eyes for her like I knew this was all so silly, all this explaining.

"Maybe it's not okay that I'm here." She was ready to go.

"I'm sure it's fine. The people whose house this is now are good people." And for some reason I went on to promise her that Ames and her husband Zebulon were good people, although I still hadn't met Zebulon, only seen pictures. On the beach, he had an immaculate, rangy, superhero's body. People with bodies like that usually aren't good people. His bathing suit, tie undone, had left red diamond-shaped in-dents in my belly.

The woman smiled. She put a hand on my shoulder for balance and with a flick of a buckle the leather crisscrossing yielded and the sandal just dropped. As soon as she had walked a comfortable distance away, Black Santa was on the sandals, sniffing fervently for information.

"I've seen those," the woman said, pointing at a lacquered stump that was acting as a coffee table. "Those are as expensive as I don't even know what. Your friends are doing okay."

I rehearsed a few snarky snipes about wealth and excess that would show I wasn't these people, but couldn't settle on one before the woman was done with the stump and moving on.

"There used to be a wall here," she waved as we walked through the living room into the dining room. "It's weird. It actually feels kind of like I'm walking through a wall. Whoa," she said, walking backwards and then forwards again through the room. "Like there's a memory of the wall here. Like a phantom limb. Oooooo." She hunched her shoulders and wiggled her fingers in a spooky way.

She had black bike shorts under her dress and tattooed lines that looked like creeping branches or sticks of lightening travelling from her ankle all the way up her calves. She turned to me and this time the hint of letters through her dressed looked like *SKILL*.

"This is so much nicer than the house I grew up in," she said, leading me through the kitchen, dragging her hands along the marble counter top. A week's worth of empties were piled by the sink, looking like I'd maybe had a party the night before. "Has it ever happened to you," she said, leaving the kitchen and heading up the steps, "that you're with a person for years and it ends and then you run into them later and they look so much better, are so much better? And you think, Why couldn't you have been this great when we were together? And you realize that they had to go through you to get better and you could just kill yourself on the spot? That's kind of how this house feels. I wish I grew up in this house. Think of the different person I would have been. But, then again, I'd've had to be a different person, have had to have had a different mother, to have grown up in this house."

She pointed out the paint job where there had been wallpaper, the new banister, the spot where her brother had run into the wall and blamed it on her, the missing wainscoting, some decorating choices that would have made her mom—she swore to God—*fucking shit*. "These photos are all so beautiful," she said, gasping, actually unhooking a frame from the wall to get a better look. "Who took these?"

"I don't know. Maybe the guy?" I didn't think that Ames had any interest in photography. I'd been there a week and hadn't taken one look at the pictures. Inspecting them now, they were all just old barns. Just old falling-apart barns in fields with big skies behind them.

"Zebulon," she said. "That's a fascinating name. Where's that from?"

"Fucked if I know," I shrugged, wanting to her to know that I could swear too.

"Well, they look like they could be in a book. I love the texture of the old wood and the flaking paint. Like they've just been ripped out of a *book*." She handed the picture to me to be rehung, and carried on down the hall. At that point it occurred to me that this woman might be crazy, and that letting her into Ames's house might have been the wrong choice.

I don't get fucked in this story, though it has all the makings of an impossible fuck story: kind of good-looking and obviously unhinged woman comes to the door, wants to take a tour of her awkward childhood. *This was my bedroom*, she says. *A lot of old memories in here*, she says, sitting down on the bed, *but how about we make some new memories?*

"They kept the claw foot tub!" the yell came from the bathroom. "The one nice thing about this place and they just knew to keep it. I used to imagine that I was taking a bath in the belly of animal!"

Not being able to line the nail with the hook on the frame, I leaned the picture against the wall instead. Black Santa peeked over the top step, her eyes wide. She hissed and ran back down the stairs and I didn't see her until the next morning when I woke up to her on my chest, staring at me like she was trying to strangle me with her thoughts. Never mind that she started out as my cat. This was her house now, and I was no better than this woman.

She came out of the bathroom and walked straight to the room I had been staying in. "This was my room," she said. "Can I go in?"

The door was open before I had a chance to answer.

For a year I lived in Montreal and worked in a small brewery that was popular enough to need to brew around the clock. On the night shift one night there was a knock at the back door. The brewer, an effete, nervous Parisian not much suited to the heavy lifting of brewing answered the knock and found a young girl in her underwear, shivering in the rain. He let her in, I'm sure thinking that this was his chance to be fucked in a scenario that was not supposed to ever happen. Long story clipped, the girl was crazy for crack and wound up stabbing the little Frenchman in an unfatal place. This is the story I thought of, slowly following the woman into her old bedroom, my current one, preparing myself to either be fucked or stabbed.

More cans of beer, these ones less organized; the ratty hand towel I had been messing nightly hung pathetically over the chair to dry; the pile of comics fallen and fanned out in the corner; a stack of sketchbooks on the desk, unopened after a week, a scattering of pens still uncapped; on the bedside table the pictures of Ames lounging on many different beaches in the same simple black bikini I had culled from the photo albums I found. The woman didn't seem to notice any of this.

"It's weird," she said. "I don't have any memories of being in here. I was never allowed to hang posters or anything. I wasn't allowed to make it mine. My bedroom growing up was basically a guest room." She walked around my room. There was a smell in there. I'd been in there a week and I had already left a smell distinct from the rest of the house, one of stale beer and body. Picking up the pictures of Ames, she flipped through them. "Beautiful," she said. "Girlfriend?"

"Was."

"I'm sorry," she said by rote, looking still at the pictures. "Wherever these places are, I want to go there. And with a body like *that*."

On the bed, the flaps open, was the DVD player box I had found that morning, hidden on a shelf behind suits in Ames and Zebulon's bedroom closet: pill bottles, nail clippers, the sharp kitchen knives, an antique pistol. In that first week, I hadn't done one lick of cooking and so hadn't noticed the lack of good knives, and my snooping hadn't led me yet to the cleaned-out medicine cabinet.

At the window she sighed, looking into the backyard. "Ohhh. There used to be *trees* out there. I don't remember what *kind* of trees. But there were two big ones. Two big leafy ones. Why would your friends have removed them? They were lovely, leafy trees."

"I couldn't say."

"I buried a time capsule back there. Not like actually a time capsule. A fucking box or something. When I was ten or something. I put pictures of myself and my friends in there. There were some poems in there and some mixtapes. I remember putting in a piece of paper with everyone I was in love with on it. God knows what else. If they dug up the tree, then they probably dug up that box."

"Makes sense."

"What would you do if you dug up something like that?"

"What would *I* do?"

"*You.* I mean *any*-fucking-body. It would be pretty awesome to find something like that. To find all these things that a person hid about themselves, but to not know the person. I wonder what your friends must think of me from the stuff in that box."

Back in the foyer, I asked the woman if she had found what she was looking for. I hadn't gotten her name, and I thought it was too late to ask. Now, through her dress, it looked like her shirt said *SKULL*.

"I don't know if I was looking for anything in particular. I just wanted to have a look. My mom died. I was in town for the funeral."

"I'm sorry."

"Yeah," she said. "It's the price you pay for leaving the house. As my mom used to say."

Something about the way she was standing made her look like she was waiting to be hugged. She was looking at me like she wanted me to look at her, but I was only looking at her bare feet. Her toes were square and all the same length. The dark diamonds left by the straps were brown in a way that could have been either tan or dirt. I looked back up to her face. Probably she was just a few paces past thirty, probably the same age I was. People my own age still looked older than I was, compared with the image of myself I had in my head, which still put me at hardly twenty. I should have kissed her. The worst thing that could have happened was she hit me. The best thing was an impossible fuck story.

"You were on your way for a swim," she reminded me. "I interrupted."

"I'll let you know if I find that box."

"Okay," she said and left.

It wasn't until the next day, when I made another limp attempt to leave the house, to go swimming in the lake that Ames had recommended—"A gorgeous bit of water that absolutely no one else in the world knows about,"—that I found Black Santa wrestling the woman's sandals in the foyer, trying to break their neck. I hid them from her and didn't leave the house that day, sat around in Zebulon's swim trunks drinking just in case that woman came back. The next day I conceded the sandals to Black Santa and set down to rooting through the house, room to room, closet to closet, cranny to cranny, looking for that box.

# BEGINNER

"All my life I wanted to *be* somebody. I realize now I should have been more specific."

–Jane Wagner, *The Search for Signs of Intelligent Life in the Universe*

One time, all Frances wanted to do was be awesome at karate. Karate would be her thing. You would look at Frances, and she would seem normal, if little, and you would never guess she could kill you in so many clean, graceful ways. Sizing up people in the street, scrutinizing them for weak points: this is how her mind would begin to work. Karate would be the new centre of Frances's life, the drain down which everything else spiralled.

This was the winter she abandoned her lit degree and the second time she'd bucked school.

So Frances signed up for a beginner's class at a dojo in a plaza along with a hairdresser's, pizza place, and dollar store, and that first class was the best thing in the world. It was bare feet and flipping people. All the ground was mats there, all the walls were mirrors, and the whole studio smelled like a high school gym class held in a call centre. Louder than any of the other beginners, France yelled "Yes, Sensei!" at wide-shouldered, gel-haired Sensei Brian like she was ready to give up her life for him.

The dojo supplied her with a crisp new karategi. All week Frances wore that gi around the house, waiting for someone to knock so she could answer the door in it. No one came by. It was exam time.

At her second class Frances was physically awkward and weak and her height was not the evasive advantage she assumed it would be. She got flipped more than she flipped and the mats weren't as soft as she thought they legally should be. The worst of it, Sensei Brian turned out to be a phenomenal asshole who used the word *faggoty* more than once and wouldn't stop staring down Frances's gi when she bowed. When she caught him he had winked and that great gi was just pajamas now.

Another time, in the messy wake of a seven-month fling with a Women's Studies major who liked to be strangled, Frances got fixed on becoming this amazing accordion player. She would play in any band around town, and be constantly on tour with whoever would have her. Off to the side and intense, accordion players were Frances's favorite, the way they leaned over their squeezebox and listened hard to the thing the way she imagined mechanics listened to engines. Using squirrelled tip money she had been saving for a possible third stab at school, Frances bought an accordion, only it never occurred to her that she would have to learn how to play the thing. Frances had assumed that it would come naturally to her, like how a baby, chucked into a pool, just swims away.

And then there were countless other times and countless other things. There were boyfriends and girlfriends, and university degrees, and philosophies both low- and highfalutin. There were trades and travel plans. And there was quitting the same café job over and over, and there were depressions that came in all kinds of sloppy, shitty, trite shades. Everything in Frances's life was adding up to something like Zeno's paradox, which Frances understood enough to know that it had something to do with moving forward but never getting anywhere.

She was ready for a meltdown at thirty, that imaginary line she had drawn between when it was okay to be a fuck-up and when it wasn't. But thirty came and went without any significant cracking, without any significant anything. A plan to move to Montreal fell through like too many groceries in a wet paper bag, and a photo essay about the fancy sneakers Southern Ontario Mennonites wore ended when Frances watched a ten-year-old Elvis impersonator get hoofed in the chest by a horse at the St. Jacobs Farmers' Market. But that spring Frances joined a queer backyard spandex wrestling league and, for a time, everything seemed stable, life seemed livable.

The panic came at thirty-one, phoning home for her birthday wishes. "It's like they say about life being like a box of chocolates," her step-mom had offered, unsolicited, while she waited for Frances's dad to come in from mowing the lawn. "Maybe your box just didn't come with one of those chocolate map-y things and you have to do little nibbles on every piece to find what you like. That's just your box of chocolates, hon." Frances had hung up. When her dad phoned back it wasn't with birthday wishes, just instructions on how Frances was to treat her step-mom, as if the woman was some easily-spooked Pomeranian with a long list of dietary restrictions.

The next night, in a weed-tizzy tinctured with too much red wine, Frances slipped away from her birthday party. After a delirious bus ride where she seriously worried about being attacked by a gaggle of sullen kids in black hoodies—where was that gi when she needed it?—she stormed the Corbet Community Centre and signed up for a beginner's art class for adults.

"Because I just feel like my whole life has just been doodling," was the reason Frances gave back at her party, purple wine smirks in the corners of her mouth, "and I want to start *drawing*, you know? Fuck."

Frances's co-workers had baked her a vagina cake. It was brought out and Frances huffed at the thirty-one candles that formed the pubic hair over the petally flourishes of pink and red icing, only they were the kind of candles that didn't blow out. Frances's bush fire just guttered and no one knew what to do.

Frances arrived for her first art class, keen as hell and a smidge higher than she wanted to be, to find a classroom of chattering children. Waiting by the door was a woman with a clipboard and rolls of masking tape on her wrists like jewelry. She wasn't wearing a bra and from a few rooms away Frances could discern the general shape of her breasts and her nipples through the hazy blouse. Up close those things were harder to make out, but still there, still obvious now that Frances knew what to look for.

"I've fudged the nights," Frances admitted. "Or I wrote down the wrong room."

The woman scanned her clipboard, clucking her tongue. She looked younger than she probably was, and had the distinct, curbside couch smell of the more free-wheeling population in town. Frances had often wondered what these people did for work, and here it was. Maybe Frances could inquire about teaching a class at the community centre. Making Bongs From Things Around the House 101. First class: An Apple a Day Keeps More Than the Doctor Away.

"You're Dr. Ludlow?" the teacher gasped, apparently thrilled that she had found the name.

Only when Frances was particularly twisted did she pretend a professional career. The night of her party was foggy, her cleanest memory being everyone burning themselves trying to take the relentless candles out of the cake. And then everyone standing around sucking their fingers. And then more wine, and some let-down mushrooms. And to end the night Frances had disastrously fooled around with a girl nearly half her age.

Bad Service, the café that Frances had been working at on and off for thirteen years, had recently hired a fresh crew of first-year university students to replace the graduates who left in the spring. Frances's party had been at the café, and the new hires had brought along all their buddies. They quizzed Frances about bands and books and movies that she had never heard of, acting flabbergasted and slighted that she was unaware, advising her with a medical severity that she really should check them out. Emboldened by whiskey, Frances started to fabricate art that she could act shocked that these kids were not experts on.

"You've never heard *Oedipus and the Motherfuckers*? Oh my god, you really should check them out." "You've never read Louis Tully? Jesus Christ, you need to track down a copy of *The Confabulators* like fucking ASAP." "How have you never seen *Elbow Kissers*? You wouldn't think that watching an old man try to kiss his elbow for two hours could be so moving, but holy fuck. I nearly fucking cried. Fucking. Cried."

By midnight Frances's friends her own age had all gone, apologizing about things they had to get up for the next day, leaving just Frances and these moody, cawing nineteen-year-olds. One kid with big boxy glasses like Frances's mother used to wear, an old Toronto Blue Jays ringer, and the left side of her head shaved, had taken a sloppy shine to Frances, had kept winking at her.

Around dawn, as she was bluntly kissing this youth back at her house, Frances had wondered what she'd even been doing in 1991, while this kid whose hand was now starting to rub her crotch like a migrained temple was being born. Watching *The Cosby Show* probably, like everyone else, except more alone and more cynically and, eventually, a bit drunk and in love with Denise Huxtable.

In the heat of what Frances assumed had been passion, or what was supposed to look and sound like passion, this teenager had moaned "Teach me!"

Before Frances could ask, this girl, Betsy—who could probably still count how times she'd been drunk—started fumbling clothes off, snagging feet and catching earrings. "I want you to teach me stuff," Betsy said, trying to do a sexy voice while struggling with her own bra. Frances hadn't even decided yet whether she wanted this to be a no clothes thing or not.

"What do you mean *teach* you stuff? What *stuff*?"

Betsy nudged at Frances's breast with her foot and winked. "I want you to show me *whatever* you want me to know about."

And that's when Frances sobered enough to understand

that this girl believed she was with an older, travelled woman. She expected Frances to impart her years of bawdy wisdom all over her body, a bit chubby with baby fat still. But what the fuck did Frances know about sex? Fifteen years on the job and all she had figured out was that the people who think they know what they're doing, or have a store of *stuff* that they do, are the creepiest, and are probably bored with sex. These people just want at your bum. What the fuck did Frances know about anything for that matter? In the end, she and Betsy had done some pedestrian, Junior High-grade stuff until Betsy left to puke.

"That's me," Frances agreed with the clipboard. She smiled at the art teacher, and the art teacher smiled back. She was one of those local hippies who, though they didn't shave their legs and were covered with as many as seven scarves at one time, had perfect white teeth and carefully shaped eyebrows.

"And Frances is on her way?" The teacher looked past Frances, down the hall, still smiling.

"Frances?" Frances glanced over her own shoulder, half expecting to see herself, dawdling, bent at the water fountain.

"Your daughter."

Frances looked again down the empty hall.

With a peach pit chin Frances admitted that she was Frances. And in a choked hush she did her best to explain about doodling vs. drawing, and Zeno, and a little bit about karate and the summer she had decided to be a carpenter but walked out the first night after seeing some guy get the drawstrings of his shorts caught in a machine and his crotch nearly mangled.

"All I want for my life right now," she explained, whispering and harried, "is to make things look like what they're supposed to be. That's all."

Marilyn—that was the teacher's name—smiled wider. Her teeth were perfect. The kind you just wanted to lick. "It's fine by me if you join the class," she said, putting her hand on Frances's shoulder, exposing a bristly armpit, "But it's not entirely up to me, doc." And then she winked.

The class was all ponytails, baseball hats, and track pants. A dozen nine- and ten-year-olds were seated around four large teacher's desks pushed together. The clamour of them stopped when the door opened. They eyed Frances as she took a seat in their midst, most of them breathing out of their mouths and not blinking enough.

Frances waved demurely. She felt awkward and overdressed, and maybe higher than she'd first thought. She had braced herself to be the youngest in a class filled with bored, chatty middle-aged women, the kind of women she imagined took beginner art classes. Those idle women who always came into Bad Service in groups of ten, who raved for hours over glasses of wine, and then wanted to pay individually on debit. "It says option for tip on here," they'd squint at the machine, never bringing their glasses for some reason, "Is there an option to not?" Maybe because of her size, these woman had always treated Frances like a child, so for their imagined sake she had tried to put on the airs of maturity. A dour plum skirt, a limp brown sweater, saddle shoes, and a pair of glasses without a prescription.

"So there's been a mix-up," Marilyn started, and went on to explain the gist of Frances's predicament. The kids looked at her like she was something on TV.

And then Frances was put to a vote. The class buried their heads in their arms while Frances and Marilyn watched. The room smelled like old rulers and pencil shavings. At a distance again, in the unflattering greeny light of the fluorescents, Frances got a clear enough look at her new teacher's boobs to give a description to a police sketch artist.

While the children were nestled in the crooks of their arms like sleeping pigeons, it occurred to Frances that now was a ripe time to secret around the room and steal all of their little knapsacks. What did they have in those bags? Dolls? Stickers? Cellphones and computers? What did kids do with themselves these days?

Her wandering, criminal eyes caught Marilyn's. The woman winked again at Frances, as if she was on board with the whole knapsack stealing idea. They'd split the haul.

Like high-fiving and skateboards, winking seemed to be making a comeback, Frances was starting to notice. What exactly was she supposed to understand? All a wink was confirming was that the other person knew what was going on. But if you don't know what they know, or what they think you know, then a wink means nothing.

At the vote, all the hands had gone up in favour of Frances—except one. One hand couldn't stay down enough.

After class Frances scanned the parking lot for that kid, that redhead with a melon as big as a pumpkin that for the rest of the night had stared hatefully at her like he was trying to blow her up with his mind. After outlining the course—a two month trajectory from The Basics and The Fundamentals to the final Secret Project!!!!—they had gone around the table for introductions. "I'm fickle Frances," Frances had offered, "and my favorite food is foie gras." The kids had really tittered at that one, whatever it meant. "I'm just Derek," the redhead complained when it was his turn, "and I don't like any foods that start with d, okay?"

At the very least, Frances wanted to get a look at the poor woman who had squeezed that impossible skull out of her body. But the lot emptied and there was no sign of Derek.

In her car she fixed a modest bowl. Pulling out, Frances watched the community centre get small in her rearview mirror, liking the feeling of leaving a place having done something there. Things were changing, it felt like. Finish this class and she could finish any goddamned thing. If Frances could get control of her life metaphorically, then handling the real meat of it shouldn't pose a problem.

"You know a gal can't live on metaphor alone," one of the teenagers from Bad Service had warned Frances the night of her party. But Frances wasn't so sure. She had lived alone for a while now.

She passed him sitting on the curb by the bus stop. Her Honda's one working brake light turned Derek an evil red. As she backed up, Frances tapped her pipe into an empty coffee cup. "Need a lift?" she called out, leaning across the front seat.

Frances's logic explained to her that because she was a woman, and a woman in the same art class as this kid, bringing Derek into her car was not inappropriate and in no way pedophiley.

After looking down the street for any hint of the bus, Derek stood up like he had no other choice, like he'd been caught running away from home.

"I know that smell," Derek said at the open window. He stared cruelly at Frances, half in the dark of the night, half in the light of her car, that same head-exploding intensity from class. Finally he said, "You don't need those to see."

Frances took off her glasses and handed them across the seat to Derek, who put them on and looked around, then took them off and looked around, then put them back on and burned at her through them.

"I could tell the way you looked through them in class that you didn't need them. People who need glasses don't like wearing them. That's how you can tell. If they didn't have to then they wouldn't."

"Maybe I like the look of them," Frances said.

"So say I think wheelchairs looked really cool," Derek started, sounding out his idea, "and what if I just started going around in a wheelchair because I liked the look of it? Because I liked how it looked on me?"

"I don't think that's the same thing."

"I don't know if it is," he said, getting into the car. He looked at himself in the side mirror, then handed the glasses back to Frances. Opening the glove compartment to stow the glasses, her knuckles brushed Derek's crotch. Frances flinched, but the boy didn't seem to notice. His thighs were soft and white in a way that made her want to slap them raw and purple.

"Sorry about the state," she said when Derek began to collect the mess of library books from around his feet, piling them on his lap. The books were at various stages of overdue, from really to extremely to shockingly, but Frances kept paying the fines. Her interest in astrophysics, or the Bolshevik Revolution, or post-colonialism, or masonry would be repiqued every time the library phoned asking for their books. "*I know* it would be cheaper to just buy them," Frances sassed back when the librarians phoned. "Don't you think I don't know that?"

"You've read all these?" Derek asked.

"You betcha." Frances pulled away into a red light.

He opened a book and leafed through. He settled on a

page.

"Okay," he said. "I am a small songbird. I have a pale brown back, a black face patch, a black chest patch, and a yellow or pale throat. I have small horns on the top of my head and the sound I make goes 'su-weet.' What bird am I?"

"I don't know." The light greened and Frances was off. Coming down one side of the street was a girl she worried might be Betsy, but she couldn't tell any of these kids apart. They all had tight jeans and dock shoes and moved with the same sort of offended insouciance. "Are you a Patchy Sweeter?"

"I thought you said you read this book." Derek scowled at Frances.

"I've started," Frances said. "I just haven't got to that part yet."

"A right here," he said, turning away and looking out the window. Frances stifled an urge to knock on his skull, test his ripeness.

From then on the only talking Derek did was calling out the turns, until he had directed Frances into an end of town she didn't know had houses. "So, what are your parents up to tonight?" she wanted to ask, but resisted.

Murder flitted to mind. She had this kid. Really had him. Do people murder people because they really mean to, she wondered, or because the opportunity's there? When she was little she would marvel at her cat, Althea, how frail and trusting she was. She would pet the cat's skull, place her palm over the cat's whole head, and wonder how easy ending the thing could be.

"Take this left and just drop me off at the corner," Derek ordered. "I don't want you to know exactly where I live."

"In case I'm looney toons."

"Right." He got out, only to shove his head back in. "I don't want you following me," he reminded her, and then slammed the door.

Instead of turning around Frances went forward and, after two turns, was completely lost. Every house looked the same and none of the streets seemed to have anything close to ninety-degree corners. One street just rolled into the other. Who were all these people and how did they get here and what did they do? The air of her high was starting to turn dense and sour and Frances started to seriously worry about how irrevocably lost she was.

The last time she had been this far out the land was fallow fields, crumbling sheds, and barns with mattresses, condom wrappers and empties in them. But now a whole new town was here. A Wal-Mart had been built. All the Marilyns in town had fought to keep the store out, arguing that it would take business from the independent stores downtown, but now the sprawl had gone so wide that there were plans for a second Wal-Mart. The hippies were protesting that now too. But for what? Would another Wal-Mart take away business from that first Wal-Mart?

After ten minutes of hopeless, random turning, Frances spotted a body ahead of her at the bus stop. She slowed to ask directions. Derek glanced up from the book he was reading and squinted into her approaching lights.

After that first class, Frances started seeing Derek everywhere, always dressed in high-riding track shorts and grocery store T-shirts covered in expressions like Wicked! and Cool Dude! and Totally Awesome! First she spotted him delivering papers across town from where she had dropped him off the week before. Up the opposite side of the street he came, walking in rollerblades, a canvas newspaper bag slung over his chest and a cart rattling behind. Later that week she caught him downtown, waiting for a bus and reading the free real estate listings. Sitting against the wall of the bank with the paper on his knees, Frances glimpsed the white of his underwear in the scoops of his shorts. Another time, walking back from breaking up with a guy she'd been on a few dates with—who had accused Frances of only loving things about people and not the people themselves—Frances saw Derek coming out of a women's clothing store carrying two heavy bags, a half-wrapped candy bar dangling from his mouth. She would drive or bike by bus stops and, one time out of five, he would be on the curb, bowed into a book, always alone. And he picked at his penis a lot, Frances noticed. She'd seen little boys mindlessly do this, but it seemed an odd thing for a boy Derek's age to be unconsciously up to.

Frances also started to see Betsy everywhere. Before her party Frances had never seen this girl, but now she was around every corner, always in some new ugly, sarcastic ensemble right out of Frances's grade two class photos. She was never with less than two people, some dressed like squeegee kid anarchists, some like moms from the early 80s, some like they had come from what people in the 60s thought the future would be. They dragged their feet like they'd had a long day at work, though Frances just assumed these teens never did anything. They were in bands that had silkscreened T-shirts but no songs.

When Frances couldn't duck Betsy, they had awkward conversations, Betsy inviting Frances to punk shows and zine fairs that Frances wouldn't be caught dead at, or at least felt too old for. When Betsy and her friends were obviously stoned or drunk, Frances found herself disapproving, even if she was one or both of those herself. She escaped away with an excuse of somewhere she had to be. Her stepsister's ex-husband's dog was graduating from obedience school, she had to pick up her car from the mechanic's, she was late to visit old friends at their new yurt in a part of the outskirts that had yet to be built up.

Whatever Frances's reason, Betsy responded the same. "Awesome," she'd drone, from the back of her throat. "Oh, cool." Frances was furious with herself for doing the things she had done with Betsy. That was not what she needed to be doing at this point in her life. At the very least, she should be going down on strangers with mortgages.

The other person she was seeing more of around Corbet was Marilyn, strutting in her flowing, gaudy hippy dresses, gesticulating wildly while speaking softly, usually in the company of men with beards or women as crunchy and effusive as she was. Twice, Frances had spotted her teacher topless in the streets, a legal though rarely acted upon way for women to walk around in Ontario. Whenever she noticed Frances she would wink in a way that felt the same as a blown kiss.

All the teens at Bad Service thought it was an absolute scream that Frances was taking an art class with children. "That's *so* cool that you're doing that," they said. "Oh my god." And in a way it was. Frances wasn't blind to that. She could remember being their age, in that frame of mind, where all that mattered was how interesting the things you were doing or the things you knew about were. Never mind whether you were any good or successful at those things or not. The people she had admired most when she was that age were the ones who landed a job being a butler for eccentric local millionaires who took them on winter vacations, or those who participated in demolition derbies for the blind up north some weekends, or who knew people in New York. If you couldn't tell some outrageous story about what you'd done, what was the point?

Children or no children, the art class was hard. This she didn't mention to the teens. Frances hated how hard it was, hated that that made her want to quit. She didn't have the patience to sit at a desk with a ruler and complete her perspective drawings, or make a gridded oval every time she wanted to draw a face. She thought she'd signed up for an art class, not a planning-to-make-art class. Getting a bit high would briefly do the trick, but Frances could only manage to get a few lines and a couple shapes onto the page before the bird of her attention winged off to another project. The rest of her homework night Frances would spend reading ten pages of a book about Wyatt Earp, or cutting out pictures of fat, bald, professional men for a folder she was compiling, or watching some David Lynch shorts that the video store really wanted back.

The weeks passed and Marilyn's lessons became increasingly New Agey, having less to do with the technique and practice of art and more to do with the technique and practice of living. Like figure drawing. While sectioning a head into four hemispheres filled with circles, squares, and triangles, trying to get the class to see complicated figures as being made up of simple shapes, Marilyn paused to point out that this artist's trick could just as easily be applied to the tricky intricacies of life. When she drew on the board, her breasts would waggle furiously and obviously under her shirt.

"When you think about it," she paused to say, her cans

swaying to a halt, "we're really all made up of the same basic shapes, aren't we?" And then that wink of hers, aimed always at Frances. What could this woman possibly know about life if she didn't even know that she was showing her tits off to a class full of children? That only certain dads could pull off a wink?

"Fucking hippy-dippy fucking bullshit," Frances called the approach one night after work in a Jägermeister rage. "What that woman needs is a bra and punch in the fucking face."

Marilyn never checked their homework—"Draw a portrait of someone you admire. Draw a portrait of someone you don't know. Draw a portrait of someone from your imagination."—so Frances stopped doing hers. She would burn whole classes scribbling and making lines in her book to keep up the appearance of work, all the while flip-flopping whether she should just get up and leave. She could lose fifteen minutes ogling Marilyn's chest, getting winked at when she was caught. Whenever she resolved to take another crack at it, to do the work, Frances would freeze up, spend a whole class staring back at the one eye she had managed to put on a page. If she'd got brave enough to try another eye, she wound up with tits basically. Maybe the incessant presence of Marilyn's breasts were somehow gumming up Frances's imagination.

It didn't help seeing how dedicated and accomplished the children were, how not hesitant. They would squint at their blank page for a few minutes, spin it around on the table to see different angles of attack, and then jump at the task. They twirled and chewed their hair while they drew, they sang to themselves, they made quiet farting noises with their mouths. When Derek drew his tongue came out and slopped all around his lips in a way that would have been pervy if he hadn't been a little boy.

Presumably to guard his beeswax, Derek would sometimes prop two binders in front of him, but always his eyes were peeping over top, seething at Frances. His was the dense, fixed, ireful glare of a cat watching a bird through a window.

The teens at Bad Service were all certain Derek was in love with her. They wanted her to take him on a date at the café so they could meet him. "He totally sounds like one of those Glass kids," they droned. But Frances wasn't so sure Derek's feelings towards her were positive, never mind loving. He seemed constantly offended by her, like someone watching an adult hit a child in the mall, so horrified that he couldn't turn away. Frances couldn't figure him out, couldn't solve the mystery of him.

To open every class the kids and Frances got out their sketchbooks and took up whatever utensil they wished, then closed their eyes. On an old boombox, Marilyn played a mix of vigorous and dolorous classical music or else plodding, whiny folk. Eyes clamped, the class responded. The point was to unfetter creativity, a stretch before a workout. Frances found it entirely useless, so she kept her eyes open. She watched the kids work. At times they would get so into the warm-up that their whole bodies bobbed and shifted, a blind wobble very close to the movements of Stevie Wonder and Ray Charles. Frances had never been that committed to anything.

Keeping her eyes open reminded her of balking grace when she was little, being the only one at the dinner table looking, watching her step-mom's lips work as she prayed. Frances wasn't the only one who thought this granola free-for-all was bullshit. His eyes just visible over the line of binders, Derek was always watching.

Frances fancied that they shared an attitude towards the class, towards Marilyn, towards life. Over the weeks, the kids in the class had gotten to know each other, had formed friendships, but Derek had kept to himself. All the time he looked serious, insular, and brooding. He arrived without talking to anyone and left without talking to anyone. At the end of the night she'd watch for him in the parking lot, hoping to give him a lift like that first night. She wanted to pick his brain, if not crack it open and root around inside, just to get some clue of what his feelings about absolutely anything were. But Derek always managed to slip away.

Whatever was up that boy's craw, investigating it was enough to keep Frances coming back to class each week. She had pretty much given up on all the art stuff. Nothing she did would ever look like what it was supposed to be. More than anything, she wanted to get a look at the work Derek was doing. He drew much more intently, much more seriously than the other kids. There was lots of furious erasing. He would pause sometimes, stare seriously at Marilyn, as if for inspiration, and then set back down to work. Whether to sharpen her pencil or to go to the bathroom, Frances found as many excuses as she could to get up and pass over Derek, to sneak a peek at what he was drawing. But, hidden by binders, hidden by his hunched body, she could never get a glimpse.

That figure drawing lesson had spent what little patience Frances had left for the class. While the kids did geometry along with Marilyn, Frances imagined the conversation she would have with her after class: The world is not simple, she would start. If Marilyn had such a boner for unbridled expression, then the last thing she should be teaching these kids was that their lives are just a simple mingling of blunt pieces. For their lesson on drawing from life, Marilyn advised the class not to worry about getting all the details of a thing, but just the important ones, the ones that implied the other ones. Frances planned to tell Marilyn that all details were important, that real life was a muddle of detail, a fucking disaster of detail. To do justice to reality, the artist's job was to render the mess they observed, not pick and fucking choose. Maybe she'd throw a Goddamnit in there. Or maybe she'd fucking wink.

Impatient mothers outside the door brought the class to an end. Over the shuffle of bags being packed and zipped, Marilyn explained that their homework for the week was to choose one verb and, however they saw fit, draw its conjugation. Frances made a beeline for the teacher—she would address her as Miss Voss: "Listen, Miss Voss, about your class..." Or, "Listen, Miss Voss, about reality..." Or maybe, "Listen, Miss Voss, about your mammaries..."—but instead rushed out when she saw that Derek had already gone.

The evening before, Frances had been biking home from a book club where none of the members had read the book. Everyone had brought wine as their potluck contribution, and after discussing a glass more than she should have on an empty stomach, Frances consented to a haircut that came out too short, a pixie cut that made her look ten. A girl who annoyed everyone else in the group had picked up a curl of Frances's hair, puckered her lips, and made a mustache. And then everyone in the book club had mustaches, but started to feel sick and so dispersed early. Spotting Betsy coming up the street with a few professorial-looking friends on skateboards, Frances had cut into a park.

Rumbling along the grass, she found herself about to bike into the outfield of a baseball game. She dismounted and walked the long way around the diamond. Henderson's Waste Disposal was playing Bilson's Construction. On the Waste Disposal's bench Frances spotted a stressed mesh-back hat held together by a diaper pin that stuck out amongst the row of regular-sized heads. Coming up behind him, Frances pressed the button of Derek's hat with her thumb.

Derek shook his head furiously and spun around, daggers in his eyes. The heads of Derek's team bobbled around to look, too.

"I'm sorry," Frances said. She wanted to grab him by the face and kiss him.

"Oh. It's Fickle Frances," he said flatly. "You cut your hair. And grew a mustache."

"How many homeruns have you hit so far?"

Derek leaned toward Frances's body and sniffed. "I know that smell," he said.

"Are your parents here, slugger?" she asked. She scanned the crowed of parents, standing and talking to each other, chasing younger siblings around, or sitting in lawn chairs reading thick spy novels. No one who looked responsible for Derek.

"No," he said. "Tonight's wok cooking."

"When are you up?" Frances didn't believe him, but whatever the reason his parents weren't there, it was sad that they weren't. In all the weeks of class she had been mystified and sort of annoyed by him, but she'd never thought to feel sorry for the kid.

"Next."

"Oh good. Because I'm dying, right? Is the thing. And I was hoping you could knock one out of the park for me, save my life. How about it?"

"We'll see," he said.

"Su-weet," Frances said, pressing the button of his hat again.

Frances clanged to the top of the small metal bleachers and sat. Fixing a rolling paper between the pages of a book on cabinet making, Frances made a small joint for the remainder of her ride home. She peeled off her mustache and let it propeller under the stands with the cigarette butts and glass.

The batter before Derek put the ball into left field and loaded the bases. After taking a few practice swings, Derek shuffled to the plate, dragging his aluminum bat behind him like a toddler dragging a stuffed animal by the leg. The crowd, the ones who were paying attention, cheered. In place of a batter's helmet like the rest of his team had, the coach had wedged a glittering red motorcycle helmet onto his skull.

The first perfect pitch Derek ignored, and did the same when the second lobbed by. Come the third, Derek listed his head over the plate. The ball ricocheted off the motorcycle helmet and back over the cage. A fat woman tipped her lawn chair, dropping her novel, getting out of the ball's harmless way.

Beside her car now, Frances saw the bus pull up and Derek lumber on. "Follow that bus," she said to herself, engaging the ignition and taking off after him. She was dead set on seeing where he actually lived. The extremes of her imagination had him in a mansion with a wealthy and cold family, or some violent, drunk uncle in a shack by the river.

Through a few intersections and stops that weren't his, Frances rode the bus's tail, but stomped the brake to avoid running over a cat that trotted languidly into the road. While the bus turned right, the cat sat down and licked its chops, the car's headlights shining deep into the green underwater caves of its eyes. Frances gave her horn a toot, but the cat only blinked dozily like it didn't understand what she wanted from it.

When she got out of the car the tabby bobbed towards Frances with the eagerness of recognition. She bent down and offered a finger, which the cat sniffed from a few different angles and gently nibbled at before thrusting its head into her palm. The cat had a tag with a skull and crossbones on it, and on the back a stamp of "Motherfucker." The address was halfway across town.

Motherfucker continued to purr as Frances picked her up and placed her in the passenger seat. The cat took a few concerned sniffs at the mug of ash tapped out from Frances's pre-class hoot before crawling into the backseat to explore the rubble of books. As they drove, Motherfucker came back up to the front seat and looked out the window at the neighbourhoods rambling past, from time to time being caught in her own reflection.

A wealthy girl that Frances had gone to elementary school with had lived on Motherfucker's block. Frances had attended a birthday party there and cried until the girl's parents, apparently unable to contact Frances's parents and too drunk to drive her home themselves, called a cab. She was dropped off at an empty, locked house. None of the girls at Bad Service had been alive then, neither had Betsy, and Derek had been so far off. The Gadets, the neighbours to the right side of the house weren't home, and the Greens, to the left, terrified Frances. There were stories around school about the oldest son, Ronny, who supposedly went around stealing girls' private parts—whatever that meant. Hiding in a tree fort in the backyard Frances had cried, and pissed herself, and fallen asleep. She woke up in her bedroom the next morning with a twenty dollar bill under her pillow. From the Apology Fairy, her parents claimed.

The neighbourhood was a mix of ivied, pillared century homes with newer houses crammed onto what used to be the spacious single lots. Motherfucker's address turned out to be one of the old, elegant houses, though when Frances pulled up to it she spotted vines of old Christmas lights winding along the eaves and a pot leaf flag hung in one of the top windows.

Motherfucker's soft motor kept running in Frances's arms as she got out of the car, but as soon as the house came into view the tabby started to squirm, fidget, and grumble. Frances struggled with Motherfucker like she was too many bags of groceries, until the cat swatted and caught her nose. Frances opened her arms to let her drop.

Motherfucker hit the ground running and galloped away into the dark.

"Motherfucker!" she wanted to call out into the night after it, but didn't, though the light in the window with the pot leaf in it came on, as if she had.

Frances was taking a break from pot, so she was getting drunk on her day off. All afternoon she had been dismantling an old rotary phone and gluing the guts of it onto a slate of wood she found in the shed out back. She was always coming up with plans for that shed. Clear it out and turn it into a workshop, or a small gallery for local artists, or it could be a jam space where she could learn the accordion already, or a rival karate studio, or a detective agency just to see what would happen. She could learn how to fix bikes—she had a book on bikes from the library that was about half a year overdue—and then she could fix all the bikes that had been abandoned in there over the years by her many roommates, and give them away. Frances had gone out to the shed to start on one of those plans before class that night, but found the phone and the wood in there and did that instead.

Break the phone down into its smallest pieces and then present the individual simplicity of this complicatedly simple machine by naming each doodad, thingamabobber, and whatchit by its right name. That was the idea. Except Frances had no idea what any of the pieces were actually called so she quit. With time still before class, she tucked into another bottle of wine, changed into her gi, and fell asleep on the couch watching a VHS of *Golden Girls* episodes.

Ringing woke her up. Briefly, Frances stared, groggy and amazed, at the eviscerated phone on the coffee table. The living room had been practically aglow when she fell asleep, but was blue and eerie with streetlights now. More awake, Frances picked up the cordless next to her art project. On the other end was the noise of a bad connection.

"Hello?" a small voice ventured out of all that wind.

"Hello?"

"You weren't in class tonight."

"Derek?" There was surge of complicated clatter.

"It's my tenth birthday this weekend," the little voice said. "I handed out invitations tonight. You weren't there."

"I guess I was sick."

"So do you want to come to my party? It's Saturday. At my house."

The address Derek gave was only a few blocks from her own, on the opposite side of town from where she had dropped him off.

"There'll be prize bags," he said, and hung up.

Frances dialled the number back. She let it ring until someone picked up.

"Derek?"

"This's Ben," the someone said. In the background, a clatter and cheer, and the incoherent sound of music being played too loudly. "Who is this?"

"Frances?"

"Want to come bowling, Frances?"

"Ben?"

"Yes, Frances."

"There isn't a redheaded kid there with a head the size of a boulder, is there?"

"Don't see one," Ben said.

"Okay. Never mind."

"Frances?"

"Yes Ben?"

"I was on my way to go pee and this phone was ringing so I picked it up and I answered it."

"Thanks for answering, Ben. Have a good pee."

"You too, Frances. Come bowling. Everyone's here."

Frances hung up and decided to go to the alley and find Ben. She pictured him in his mid-twenties, gel-spiked hair and too much cologne; a polo shirt and khakis guy. They would hit it off but they wouldn't keep in touch. The night would just be this weird, remarkable, fun thing that happened to the both of them, on a lark. Then she would join a bowling league. She would book Sunday mornings off from Bad Service for games. The owner would understand. She would buy custom shoes, and one of those wrist guard things—whatever those things were. She would get her own fancy ball, maybe sparkling and vibrant like Derek's batting helmet. And she would get to know all these men she would not otherwise know. Men with big, hard stomachs, and mustaches. And she would get to know their lives, and their families, and she would start playing softball with them too. They'd start her off in the outfield, but gradually she would work her way up to becoming the star pitcher—Fireball Frances. Scouts would start showing up to games, watching her closely, whispering to one another, making cramped notes in their little notebooks.

Instead, Frances rewound her *Golden Girls* tape to the beginning.

The only hint of a party at the address Derek had given was an orange balloon tied to the hook of the mailbox. It lolled on the porch with the same spits of breeze that seemed intent on lifting Frances's party dress. There didn't seem to be anybody home, never mind a kid's party raging. For years the neighborhood had been something of a slum, the houses sectioned into apartments in which dead bodies were sometimes found. But now families were moving back, and the houses were being restored. Derek's house, or the one he claimed was his, had an awkward look, like a pair of cut-off jeans that had had the legs sewed back on.

Frances made up her mind that this party was all a trick and decided to go home, where she could smoke an apple and lay carpet in the shed. Instead she went up and knocked. She had bought a present and a new dress, after all. In a vintage boutique, Frances had fingered the racks of the children's section and found some options, most of which, when she tried them on, looked more slutty than cute, settling at last on a bland mauve dress with shapes on it that looked like flowers if you weren't looking. Paying for the dress, Frances had spotted the perfect gift for Derek on the shelf behind the cash.

Peering through the cup of her hands, Frances could make out nothing through the bevelled glass. With her ear against the door now, she rang the bell and waited for sound.

Something hit her between her shoulders and she jumped, dropping Derek's present. "Fuck you!" Frances yelled out. Reaching around, she grabbed for the arrow or the knife or for whatever the fuck might be sticking out of her back.

Derek was at the bottom of the concrete steps, arms limp at his sides. A hot pink plastic bird the size of a mouse lay there on the porch. Frances picked it up and shook her fist. "I'm keeping this," she seethed at Derek, trying to crush the thing in her hand. The beak and feet just dug in.

"It was for you anyway. Everyone gets one."

"Well I'm still keeping it."

Party or no party, Derek was dressed for one. He had on what appeared to be a crinkly plastic Dracula cape and two pointed party hats on either side of his head, making horns. The T-shirt he had tucked into his swim trunks read *It took me 50 years to look this good.*

"Happy birthday," Frances said.

"I didn't do anything." He took a few urgent pinches at his crotch.

"Then where's your mother? I'll congratulate her."

"She's out. Her and my dad. They went out to pick up the clown and the magician. Their car broke down."

"The clown and the magician were coming in the same car?"

"I guess." Derek walked up the steps, his cape luffing behind, and picked up his present. "This is mine?"

"Maybe." The only thing Frances had around the house

that resembled wrapping paper was tinfoil. The present glinted in Derek's hand like a piece of some crappy spaceship.

"Is it a book? Or is it one of those things where I'm supposed to think it's a book but that's only to throw me off the trail of what it really is?"

"You'll have to open it to see."

"I'll put it with the rest."

"Where's everyone else?"

Derek looked around suspiciously. "I don't know," he said, an impish lilt to his voice.

"I guess they could be *anywhere*," he yelled, and winked.

Derek looked at Frances looking at him, screwed up his face in imitation. "If you're not careful," he said, "your face will stick that ugly way."

Frances followed him into the house. It didn't smell like a boy lived here. The place had the smell of cardboard and potpourri. She imagined a trembling elderly couple bound and gagged in a closet somewhere. Hung low on the foyer wall was a framed picture of Derek with Shania Twain. Shania had been caught in a blink and Derek was holding a baby like he was asking the camera what it was. His smile looked out of place. Frances had only ever seen a grimace carved into his pumpkin. She pressed her thumb on Derek and then considered the patterned haze she had left over his face.

"I didn't know you knew Shania."

"She smelled like old macaroni," he called from the other room.

In the living room she found him on his hands and knees, lifting up the flaps of the couch. He had taken off his sandals where the hallway linoleum turned to salmon-coloured carpet. Frances slipped her own sandals off.

She wanted to bend down and pet him like a cat.

"I can get up fine on my own," Derek said, looking at Frances's outstretched hand. With a put-upon sigh, he stood up and dusted off his hands like he had been fixing the couch.

"Did you lose something?"

"I'll lose it on you if you want."

The living room was stale and staid like a department store. Innocuous pastel floral patterns covered the surface of the room and the carpet looked and felt like it had hardly been walked on, except for a few slithering lines that had been gouged into it. Frances imagined Derek rolling through the house on the rollerblades she had seen him delivering papers in.

"So this is where you live?"

Derek put his finger to his lips and kissed it viciously. He pointed at the curtains and nodded at Frances. Frances nodded back. And she tried winking. Derek tiptoed to the curtains and poked his head behind, then submitted himself completely.

"So you weren't there for it, but Marilyn gave us our final project last class." There was a disturbance behind the curtain, like he was wrestling with something back there, but then the fabric settled. Derek's toes, pale baby carrots, stuck out from under the hem. "She says she wants us to draw what we want in life. She says that all she wants it to be is true."

Derek came out the other end of the curtain, and Frances half-expected him to have performed a costume change.

"'All it has to be is true?' What does that even mean?"

"If you'd gone to class, you wouldn't have to ask. Sheesh. She said that there's no such thing as good. She said that we have to stop worrying about if something is good or bad, and just do it true."

"Oh please."

"What?"

"Don't you just hate that?"

"Hate what?"

"Marilyn. All her hippy shit. Don't you just hate her?"

"No," Derek said. He stared at her, and blinked.

"I love Miss Voss," he said, in a kid way, where he didn't seem to mean that he liked her a lot, or liked her class a lot, but that he actually loved her in a sincere way. "You don't like the class?"

He passed Frances, slipped his sandals back on, and went into the dining room where he bent slightly to look under the table, and then parted a fern in the corner. Carrying on into the kitchen, he opened up all the drawers, and the oven, peeping into all these nooks. Frances kept on him. On the fridge there were seven little magnets with the days of week on them, each pinching a twenty-dollar bill.

"Derek," she said, "about that class."

"What about it?"

"Well, to tell you the truth—" She had imagined quitting the class as being a crushing blow to this kid. Maybe the Bad Service teens were right and Frances was his first love. Maybe his cagey-ness had everything to do with the awkwardness of being enamored with an older woman who was showing a consistent interest in him. Maybe she was a replacement for his non-existent mother. Maybe the thing he had been working so maturely on, the thing that he worked so hard to keep hidden from her, was a grand, badly drawn declaration of love. But, now that Frances was poised to tell him, it seemed likelier that he wouldn't care in the slightest.

"You've been lying to me so far?" His face took on that old, serious cast.

"No. I've... That's just a thing to say."

"What a thing to just say."

"Derek, I don't think..."

"Wait," he said. "Shh," he said. "Wait here. Don't move."

Derek winked at Frances, and with stealth and lightness passed back through the foyer, careful not to make a sound closing the door behind him. Abandoned, Frances waited. She wanted to be in the exact same position when he came back.

While she waited Frances did the math in her head. For this boy to be turning ten today he would have been born in 1999. What had Frances been doing in 1999? She didn't think she had even been on the internet by 1999. That Betsy girl would have been eight. Meaning Frances had put her mouth on the private parts of someone who had been eight at the same time that Frances had been, legally, an adult. How was that not a kind of pedophilia? What was the difference, then, between that and putting her mouth all over Derek's private parts?

Probably she had been starting her first year of university, or already a year in, doing too many chemical drugs and drinking too much, in love with bands she would never listen to again. She had lasted a year and a half in biology before becoming convinced that she wasn't learning anything. She had been dating this Gregory guy for a lot of that time and when she dropped out they moved together into a communal house with a few people and a couple families in a part of town that was all identical looking houses now. There were so many people doing so many things, all of them options. Frances could become an organic farmer, or a magician, or a social worker, or she could work in a café in Guatemala, or she could be a brewer, or a bass player, or a paleontologist, or speleologist, or who the fuck knew what. Life became so gaping and full all of a sudden. There were doors everywhere, all of them wide open. Any of these people she could be like, but Frances wanted to be like all of them all at once. Then one of the children brought lice home and everyone in the house was crawling with them. Everyone had to shave their heads. And while Frances loved how she looked with a shaved head, she hated how a house full of people with shaved heads looked.

If Frances went bald on a Friday, she had moved into her father's house on the Sunday, where she had lived for a season. She watched talk shows and read *Franny and Zooey* over and over again until she became convinced that her not understanding the stories was a kind of understanding. She got lit in the backyard while her dad was at work, found a few alien-looking fake penises in her step-mom's drawer and put the batteries upside down, and yelled at her dying cat Aleatha to get a job. And somewhere during all of this, some poor woman was forcing a football with red hair out of her strained privates.

When after a few minutes Derek didn't come back, Frances gave up not moving and went to the drawers and considered stealing a spoon. She found one like she liked, but had no pockets in her dress to hide it away in. She tried to stow it in what little cleavage she had, but the spoon fell right out the bottom of her dress. She settled on sticking it in her armpit, bending it, and then returning it to the drawer. A cough came from upstairs.

A track ran along the wall. At the top was a simple metal chair like the ones that flight attendants use. Making as little noise as possible, Frances climbed up to the chair and sat down on it. She searched for a switch to work the thing. On her knees, she saw the imprints. In the carpet there were two trails like the ones in the living room. They wended under the door of the first room. Frances got close to the wood and listened. There was the sound of a person trying not to make any noise. And maybe it was her own desire for just a little sip of some right then, but Frances was sure she could smell just the faintest hint of pot wafting from the room.

Frances curled her fingers to make a tiny, cautious knock, but instead headed for the door at the end of the hall.

A normal boy's room with A *Star Wars* poster on the wall, a few actions figures scattered on the floor that were probably being played with less and less each day, a tiny desk that was more a place to throw things than to do work at, a bed made by an adult. Frances opened the top drawer of Derek's dresser and took out a pair of underwear. Little robin's-egg-blue boy's underwear, practically panties. With no pockets to stuff the little bundle in, Frances pulled Derek's panties up over her own.

There were two framed newspaper articles hung beside the door. One had Derek smiling that same creepy smile in a heap of books. According to the caption, he had read two hundred books this summer, raising over one thousand dollars for the MS Read-a-Thon. The other announced Derek as the Corbet Mercury's Carrier of the Month for April. Derek's bio read, "Derek enjoys school, baseball and drawing! He is committed to delivering the news to you on time, rain or shine!"

Frances decided she would destroy the room. Tear the sheets from the bed, empty out the drawers over the floor, knock down his books. Instead, Frances went to the bookcase, set up just under the window, and looked at his collection. Among the *Encyclopedia Browns*, *Hardy Boys*, R.L.

Steins, and a few John Grishams and Michael Crichtons, there was the library's copy of *Beginner's Ornithology*.

She flipped through, looking for that bird Derek had claimed to be the night she drove him home, the one that went "su-weet." But most of the birds were indistinguishable, as birds do seem unless you know specifically what you're looking for. Printed in the late 40s, Frances figured a handful of the birds in the guide must have since died, eaten into extinction by neighbourhood cats, the only sign of them left in the world a stunned engraving in some overdue library book. Any beginner ornithologist learning with this book would be watching the skies and bushes for little things that had disappeared forever ago.

On the desk Frances saw, under a pile of neatly folded shirts, Derek's sketchbook from class. She slipped it out from under the clothes and considered it. The pages Derek had drawn on were wavy and thick next to the remaining, fresh pages. She could rip out all the art, scribble over every drawing, or steal the notebook and hand it into Marilyn as her own, becoming the star pupil of the class, eventually rocketing to international fame, her work lauded for its "youthful unpretentiousness."

Boobs, for pages and pages. For a month and a half, Derek had been becoming an expert in drawing boobs. He had started out with pretty simple shapes that more resembled eyes, graduating to more nuanced, shaded, weighted forms with astutely placed nipples. The sets were most obviously Marilyn's, but there were a few tiny pairs—and Frances considered that maybe she was flattering herself—that looked like her own. How see-through had anything she'd ever worn to class been? Maybe a kid could see through anything if he stared hard enough.

The window looked out on the backyard. Tables had been set up and the elms were full of fluttering, twisting ribbons. One table had a heap of gifts, another the promised surprise bags, and places had been set with plastic plates on the last. In the centre of each plate a rock had been plopped to keep it from blowing away. The white saucers shivered and squirmed with the breezes, unable to take flight.

She watched Derek wander into the yard, his cape blowing heroically out behind him. He stood and scratched his bum, looking at the empty backyard, maybe wondering why no one had come. Frances had been a little strange at that age too. She knew how hard it could be to get other kids to like you. Derek took a few mindless fondles at his penis while he surveyed his own failed grab at self-celebration.

Frances spotted the movement in the bushes at the same time Derek did. A motion towards the bush and the backyard hiccupped out the children it had been hiding. They jumped out of the landscaping, came out from behind fences, dropped from the trees. Children in good party clothes and children in regular clothes tucked in or decorated. Children from the class, children from his baseball team, and children Frances did not and should not recognize.

Pipsqueaks and squirts swarmed around Derek. His hands reaching to touch, he twirled after them, his cape sticking out and flapping. A few times he tripped and fell. His face was tangled with frustration. The kids moved and flowed like a cluster of birds, turning and swooping in weird synch. The order fell all apart, and each bit of it scattered in all directions, some kids finding new hiding spots, others clinging to the tree that must have been deemed safe. Derek was left standing alone again in the middle of the yard, having caught no one, still It.

He looked up at the house and squinted, smiling from the sun in his eyes. He saluted to block the light, and put his other hand far out to keep it more at bay. Frances ducked, sure she was caught, and dumped the sketchbook back on the desk. Derek's stolen underpants started to itch.

Cautiously, she peeked back over the sill. Derek was waving. Frances stood up to wave back, but didn't. Derek wasn't waving at her. The spastic arm, the wide smile, those were not aimed at her. Those were for whoever was at the other window, for whoever was getting high in that room down the hall. The hiding kids took this opportunity to move again, and the chase was back on.

Frances took off the underwear and stole back her overdue copy of *Beginner's Ornithology*, replacing it with the fresh copy she'd bought at the boutique. Wrapped still in the cheap splendour of the tinfoil, it could have been any book, could have been anything at all. In a hallway mirror, she straightened her dress before going out to join the party.

At the top of the stairs, Frances sat back down in the flight attendant chair. After some blind grabbing she found the controls. There was no obvious need for precaution, but Frances fastened the dangling seatbelt because it was there. It sat loosely on her thighs, adjusted for someone larger than her, so Frances cinched the belt tight against her stomach.

Pokey and jerky, the chair shunted down the stairs with a laboured, whiney hum. It went and stalled, went and stalled, and Frances waited, listening to the hum, feeling around under her for anything obviously overheating. Hovering over the steps, feeling like she was in a doctor's office without any magazines, Frances imagined the chair catching fire, the house wobbly with flames, children dying in great numbers, her life turned into running, living on the lam, the loneliness of it, assuming any number of identities and professions, letting people get close but never too close, not moving forward so much as moving away. And then the chair glitched back to life, and for a few steps everything seemed to be working like it was supposed to again.

# THE QUESTION WAS WHAT WAS COMPLICATED

"That's it," Danny blurted.

"That's it," he said again, like he was getting used to the words. Danny downed the dregs of the bottle he had been working on since switching from coffee at exactly noon. Another beer whispered open and Danny looked at Hannah for comment. He drank with a wincing determination, daring her to say something. Though Hannah had never had a problem with him drinking, lately Danny seemed to like imagining she did.

Chugging, Danny's eyes wandered impatiently from Hannah to the boy to nowhere. They lolled with the same unsettling, breathless detachment that the boy had when he gulped away on a glass of milk, like he didn't know what to do with his eyes while he was drinking. It made Hannah curious. Where did she look when she drank? It turned out that she watched inside the glass for the bottom to appear.

Bethany, Hannah's sister in B.C., had promised that a baby would be a constant, thrilling reminder of all the wonder that now-banal things had once held. More often than not, though, the boy's wonder only distracted him, and led to messes that, whether she was there to see them or not, were Hannah's responsibility. A crash would be followed by Danny poking his head around the corner, more like an older brother than the boy's father. "Han," he'd call, a lilt of tattle in his voice. "I think you'd better come have a look at this." The wonder was there, fine, but it was incessant and exhausting. At her most tired, Hannah couldn't wait for the wonder to be bled out of the boy, for the marvelous world to go dull again.

"That's it," Danny croaked through the sting of carbonation. He forced the rest down and brapped, lining this bottle up with the first. Hannah and the boy looked at Danny across the patio table, waiting to see where this was leading. Danny for Hannah was so often like a TV show that wasn't very good but that was always on, that she always watched, and loved. Even though she knew how stupid it was.

"That's it!" He shook his head and raised his shoulders, like he couldn't believe he hadn't thought of this before, that this was it. "We didn't come all the way out here to put up with this *crap*, Han. At least, *I* didn't."

This crap was the Fancy Dans, the band some teenagers down the block had put together. This crap was especially the drums. Danny had been a drummer, back in what he now called The Good Old Days, a term Hannah might have found more offensive if she hadn't been feeling the same way. And though he'd willingly moved his kit into his brother's basement two and a half years ago, to make room for the boy, he still subscribed to the magazines. Magazines for drummers with ugly men on all the covers. Large men with large arms, skinny men with large arms. A lot of them were balding, like Danny was balding. Whenever the teenagers down the street played Danny zeroed in on the drumming.

Drumming that sounded like hail falling on taut sheets of wax paper, he said.

"I'm sorry, Dan?" Hannah asked, egging. "What's *it*?"

"*That's* it, Hannah," he said, pointing the way to the noise. "Hannah," he said, "I'm going over there!"

Hannah had noticed that they said each other's names too much lately, as if they were worried they'd forget.

"To do what, Dan?" The boy's dull stare, hidden in the shade of that too-girlish sun hat Hannah insisted he wear, asked the same question. To do what? What would he do when he got there?

"Something," Danny answered. "I'm going to go over there. And do something, Hannah."

"At least put your shirt on, Dan."

He shook his shirt on over a sunburn and went without buttoning it up. Hannah watched him go, that waddling gait of his, grabbing up his jeans to better hide the shady fissure of his crack.

"What do you think, kid?"

The boy put a fist in his eye and opened his mouth wide to yawn, curling back his tongue like a cat.

Hannah made no big show of it. She just deftly pinched under the boy's tongue, taking away the marble he had stowed under there when he thought she wasn't looking. Where on earth had he found a marble? There had been no one on their property before them. It had been an empty field before. And who played with marbles anymore?

The boy frowned at Hannah. Caught, sorry, but angry all the same. Angry in the shade of his sunhat.

The crap fell away instrument by instrument. In this new quiet there was the roll of waves gripping a shore that was the Sunday sound of cars on the block.

The music started again in a burst. It carried itself pathetically up like a bird trying to get off the ground with a broken wing, and then fell apart again.

The wheezing breath of traffic. The slap-slap of kids running in the streets. The boy not taking his eyes off the hand that the marble had disappeared into.

"That's it!" That's what he would yell when he would threaten to leave for good, Danny. But he could never find a specific reason to go, for it to be it. Breaking the marriage would have been more work than keeping it, so they kept it. The only thing that had changed was now there was a reason to not go.

Hannah and the boy watched the back gate for Danny to come back through.

"What do you think?" Hannah asked the boy. "You think they've beaten up Dad?" Danny and teenagers: there was a history there.

With that baby chub he could rumple and contort his face into the most horrible expressions, and the boy did a doozy.

"Let's go see." Hannah upped the boy and canted him on her hip, slipped her sandals on. There seemed to be so much glass in the street lately. A few Friday nights ago someone had smashed the bus stop, the aquamarine glass of which still sparkled in the grass and on the curb, pretty if she didn't think about what it actually was. Hannah thought she could remember being able to walk anywhere barefoot without worry, when she was young. "Let's go see if they've killed Dad."

Who was breaking all this glass all of a sudden anyway? Or had someone stopped cleaning it up?

In a rush the racket began again.

It was Hannah who heard the sound of what at first sounded like a twig snapping in the night those few Halloweens ago. This was in the old house, back in the old neighbourhood, back in the city, back before the boy. Except it was a more full sound than a twig, more like the snap of a pane cracking under too much pressure from its frame. And then another snap.

It's nothing, Hannah had told herself, lying in bed. But answered herself that nothing was ever nothing.

"Dan," she whispered. And she poked him. "Dan," she said. "There's something."

Danny grumbled, his back to her, making more of a show coming out of sleep than was necessary. "The hell?"

"There's something out there," she said.

Hannah knew when Danny was asleep and when he wasn't, knew when he was just pretending. And how sad was that? Two people lying in bed, pretending to sleep? But maybe that was marriage. Two people pretending, together. They had been having a lot of talks lately about all the things marriage was supposed to be. Talks that Danny was never a fan of having. "I know the answer is I love you," Danny had said. "But for frick's sake, Han, I just don't know what the question is anymore."

Danny made a huffy production of getting out of bed, throwing the covers off and stomping to the window. His little flat nothing of a bum, two cold pancakes. And a little stiff shadow bobbing in front that Hannah had apparently interrupted. There was another snap as Danny parted the curtain.

"Frig you!" Danny shrieked. He was rough with the gauze of the curtain like he was trying to slam it. And he was gone out of the room. Hannah heard the dainty sounds of Danny being careful and also hurrying down the stairs. When he was genuinely, deeply mad, Danny cursed politely. Out came the frigs, and fricks, and the sheeshes. This polite rage had been one of those things that had endeared Danny to Hannah back at the start, back in The Good Old Days. But, like all the things that Hannah had loved about the guy—his drumming face, his little bum, the beginning of a bald spot on his crown—it was something he was seriously embarrassed of and humourless about, and would get furious at Hannah for finding adorable.

Hannah got up to take her own look out the window.

There were three teenagers in the street, throwing eggs. They were in the bare minimum of costume: nondescript jeans and dark sweatshirts, dollar store Halloween masks. There was a werewolf, a gorilla, and a black cat, throwing eggs.

Hannah and Danny had kept their porch light off that night, ate most of the candy themselves. Even still there had been knocking all evening. They had kept the light off because they had wanted to be alone together, tonight especially. They watched the same TV shows in separate rooms, alone together, but the light being off only seemed to make the kids knock harder and louder. And it must have really cheesed these three off.

Hannah watched. Danny appeared on the front lawn, waving his arms. Naked as a buck, with his pink pancakes, and his silly penis so small now in the cool of the night, probably tucking into his body like a turtle like it did sometimes. He waved his arms and yelled something at the teenagers that Hannah couldn't make out. Probably that that was it. "That's it!"

The way Danny was waving his arms wildly around his head looked just like when he played drum solos in the air along with drum solos on records, as if the drums were all around him. Like the drums were a swarm of bees that he was shooing gone. Once Danny had told her a dream he had where he was trapped in a strange cube of "futuristic-looking" drums and the only way to escape was to rock through. Hannah had only giggled a bit, but it had been enough for Danny to storm out, swearing to never tell her about any dreams ever again.

Probably Danny had expected to scare the kids off with his drum solo waving and his yelling about it being it. They would run off at the sight of this irate, naked man. But they stood there, listening to him and whatever he was yelling about.

One said something back. The mouth of the mask didn't move, but the gorilla face moved like there was something crawling around inside of it. Once, when she was a girl, Hannah and her sister had found a small dead fox in the woods behind their house. What looked like breathing, Bethany had explained, were the maggots milling around inside.

It took only the gorilla to throw an egg to make it okay for the other two. The werewolf and the cat, along with the gorilla, opened fire on Danny.

Danny doubled, hit in the crotch. He stumbled backwards and kept stumbling, back towards the house. An egg to the bald top of his head. He held one hand out to block the eggs, the other hand he had protecting his turtled penis. The werewolf, the cat, and the gorilla kept throwing. Though their masked faces were frozen in screams, Hannah could hear their laughing.

The front door slammed. Hannah ran down to him one step at a time, rushing but still being careful.

The baby hadn't taken was why they had kept their porch

light off. It wasn't even a baby, what came out, but it would have been. All that wet ingredient, that gory material. And they just hadn't felt like having little babies in dorky, adorable costumes coming to their house. The parents waiting at the end of the driveway.

Hannah took off her own robe and held it out to Danny. He was wiping snotty egg out of his eyes. He was doing this slow dance, this excruciating watusi. Where his penis would otherwise have been there was a hairy divot, a sort of second bellybutton.

"Dan," Hannah said, trying not to look at the hole.

"Dan," she said. She held out her silk robe for him, and they were both naked.

It looked like he was digging out his eyes, the goo of his eyes. Flecks of white shell like tiny teeth stuck to him. Danny's front was slick, his hair there matted, like that one disastrous time they had tried oils together.

The slime on Danny, the yoke. All that precious stuff inside such a weak case. The stuff that would have gone on to make a kid had just slipped out her, as though it was her fault for not holding it in there tight enough, for not wanting it in there enough. "It happens more than you think," was the best Bethany had been able or willing to offer, on her way out the door with her own children, all three of them dressed as Snow White that year. "You know Mom did it a bunch of times. So just think. Put it in perspective. If it hadn't been for those losses, she would've never had you."

"Dan," Hannah said, running her finger through the viscous mess on his face.

"Dan," she said to Danny.

"Dan. You've got egg on your face," she said.

Danny hadn't said anything, had stared at Hannah like

this was all her fault.

Hannah had looked away, but not in time to avoid seeing Danny reach down and pluck his penis back out of his body.

Slowly, the thing folded back inside.

The shattered glass looked like frost. Not even a pile Hannah could step aside to avoid, it was everywhere, glittering. She put down her squirming boy and let him toddle and stagger over the mess safely in his toy sneakers. Walking for him was still a sustained falling forward. He reached up for Hannah's hand, pretending to try to hold it. But it was the marble in there, the cat's eye he had found, that the boy was trying to get back from her and back into the safety of his mouth. She swapped the marble to her other hand and gave him the empty one. Only he didn't want it now, his mother's empty hand.

There was no music and no Danny. Hannah imagined him sitting at the kitchen table talking with these kids' parents, taking the beer he was offered, and then taking another. However many beers it took to get this noise business sorted, he'd be there all afternoon. If that's what it took.

The boy and the community had grown together. When he came out he had been a wriggling, pink thing. The boy was a grump, but what fresh human wasn't? Hannah figured that objectionable and unimpressed was the preset people came with. It was kindness, and affability, and compassion that were learned, or not. Her boy had turned from this thing with less personality than a mindless bird into this opinionated, fussy, oftentimes intentionally bad, full person. It felt like he changed overnight, her boy, just like the neighbourhood.

The new baby had been a surprise for Danny and Hannah.

The first one they had planned and striven for, like working an arduous summer job to save for some grand purchase. But finding out about this new one was like finding out about a fat inheritance left to them by a relative that they didn't even know. Danny insisted that, if all went well, they would move, raise the child out of the city.

"Because something's happening to this place," Danny said, finding that explanation enough. The day Hannah lost the baby and the night Danny got attacked had become all one incident in his mind. "It's not like it used to be," he offered, when he saw that his first reason hadn't satisfied Hannah. "It's changed."

Danny's brother turned them onto a new development on the outskirts. Theirs was the first new home sold and when they went to see where their new life would be it was the country still.

"Vertiginous is a word?" Danny had leaned in and said to Hannah.

"Vertiginous is a word," Hannah confirmed.

"This is just so frigging vertiginous," he whispered, putting his arm around her. A little in awe at all that green, all that country. Verdant was the word he had been looking for, Hannah guessed, but vertiginous was still a word. The question was what was complicated.

"Yes," she agreed, "it is that."

Danny and Hannah went ahead with the building, with the new life. To give complete attention to the pregnancy and whatever came from it, Hannah quit her job at the post office. The women she worked with, mostly widowed grandmothers who needed something to fill their days, had thrown her a party and made her a going-away cake. On the cake had been a stork dressed as a mail man, a bundle hanging from its beak that looked more like a full diaper than a baby. "I'm confused," Hannah had said when they brought it out.

"Better get used to that!" the old women laughed.

Days after Hannah and Danny were all moved in, they discovered that theirs was the first and only house built before the builders ran into building problems. The work had been forced to stop.

For what was promised to be better pay, Danny left his manager's position at the vacuum store he'd been at since Hannah had met him, and took a job in the secondhand sports equipment store his brother owned, Extra Innings. In the mornings he drove into city and drove back home in the gloaming. And Hannah stayed put, holding the boy in her as tight as she could. It seems like every time Hannah phoned the store, her brother-in-law would answer. Evan would explain that Danny was with a customer just then, or that he had gone to appraise some equipment that a high school was culling. When Danny phoned her back he asked the reason for the call. "What is it?" he asked. It baffled him that someone would call for no reason.

Friday nights he would stay at Evan's house in the city, supposedly so they could hit garage sales early Saturday morning. Evan's house was also where Danny's drums had been permanently stowed. And Evan's house was also where there wasn't a wife, anymore, where Danny and Evan could work on their music. It was with each other, and a guitarist named Nic who Hannah had been dating at the time, that they had played as Bastard Hymns. Around Toronto they had shared bills with a handful of bands that went on to various degrees of success. The best the Hymns had done was placing a song on the university radio charts.

A song that had been written by Nic, for her. "Hannah Spelled Backwards," supposedly about her dyslexia. With that one whiff of success, Nic had left the band, broken up with Hannah. These were the days Danny meant when he referred to The Good Old Days.

During one visit to the doctor's, Danny couldn't get past the word "fontanel."

"That's a weird word," he had interrupted. "Fontanel? Sounds more like a black lady doo-wopp group. *The Fontanelles.*"

"Dan," Hannah had said.

"What?" he shrugged. "'Black's' not bad is it?" He looked to the doctor. "You can say 'black,' can't you?"

For the remainder of doctor visits Danny was able to make he either stared into space, or lazily inspected the model womb. "I'd have to say," he said once to the womb while they waited to be seen, "That you've been a model womb."

Bundles of healthy, green lawn arrived on a flatbed and were rolled out like carpet for them. Their yard was green, but all around them was desert. Churned earth, chomped earth, upset earth. Hills of dirt, holes of dirt. There had been old, lost plans for some of this land to become a cemetery. Nothing further would be built until that got sorted and until then there were just all these holes. For the living, or for the dead.

"Fucking vertiginous," Hannah would say, looking out the window at the sandy wasteland. Uncertain of when they could begin again, the builders had left behind their machines. In the honey haze of morning and the muzzy redness of evening the machines were stalled, dark hulks in the distance. The dumb bulk of their bodies, the slim, hooked swanness of their necks. All those heads, all those jaws. Agape, unmoving, waiting, and pointless.

No city buses ran that far out then and Hannah relied on friends from the city to come pick her up. They were all new mothers. Had the first baby taken, Hannah would be a new mother along with them, would be going stroller jogging with them, would be going for morning coffee and discussing the effects of caffeine on breast milk with them, would be going to matinees that catered specifically to new mothers. But her friends were so consumed with all these young mother activities—somehow finding time in there to raise the children—that making it out to the outskirts always seemed impossible. So in the mornings Hannah watched TV. If it hadn't been for the boy in her, she would have had beers. In the afternoons she would step out and stroll the aimless landscape. Neon orange stobs jutting from the ground were the only suggestion that this was supposed to be somewhere. There was no sound out there. Well, there was sound: the hurry and scurry of animals, the chirp of birds, the chirrup of insects, the roll of cars on the faraway road, planes flying that she couldn't see.

Hannah climbed to the top of the dirt hills and surveyed the land. From that vantage her house did not look like the first to come. From there it looked like the last to go, the last tooth in a rotted mouth.

Once, Hannah found a cat lying on its side, breathing slowly, its mouth hanging open. It was fat and lustered like a plush stuffed animal. It had a collar on. Back when she and Bethany had found the fox, Hannah asked how her sister knew it was dead. "Because if it was alive it would be running away from us right now." Hannah crouched by the cat and watched the body move, presumably with maggots and rot gasses, never quite convinced that the thing was really dead. Amazed that the tumble of decay inside could so resemble life. She came back to that spot the next day and the cat was gone.

Hannah went to the machines. She would go and feel small next to them, feel new in the world, recent to this. She climbed on top of them, using the teeth of the tires as steps, and sat behind the controls. One afternoon she climbed aboard a machine with the keys still in it. The key chain was a little plastic gorilla, its arms up, its fangs bared, the white paint of its eyes faded and gone. She flicked the gorilla and it swayed and dangled like a hung man. She gripped the butt of the key and felt the capacity for doing wrong.

When Danny was home he was anxious and Hannah knew why. It was the distance and it was his bowels. Hannah had figured out that Danny couldn't go in the house, couldn't shit with her within nose- and earshot, even after seven years together. Back in the city he had had a ritual. Come eight o'clock he went for a drive, every night. One night she had followed him on her bike. She found his car parked at the Tim Horton's down the road. She waited twenty minutes and finally he came out without a coffee, just one of his drumming magazines rolled up under his arm, a skip in his step. So now he was squirming, holding it all in.

In all her and Danny's talk about divorce, it had never seemed like a thing they would do. Hannah wondered if it was a generational stubbornness. Her parents' generation had been so keen at making a relationship look so much like love, but had not known how to actually turn it into love. Now they all wanted out. Hannah's parents had waited for her to get married before divorcing. "We wanted to know you'd be taken care of," they'd said. Growing up watching that, suffering it, Hannah's generation seemed dead-set on learning how to be happy living miserably. It didn't have to look like love, it just had to be love. In his way, Danny had been right about their marriage. The answer was easy, was love, but the question was what was complicated.

"How do you and Brian do it?" Hannah had asked her sister. Whenever she talked about her husband Brian it sounded like she was complaining about some friend who had been crashing at her house for fifteen years, putting a baby in her from time to time and letting the dishes pile up.

"Do what?"

Every day for two weeks Hannah returned to that giant claw with the keys still in it. She went and she sat behind the brains of it, tickling the gorilla, pinching the key. She felt urgent there, tense. There was a tightness inside which she imagined helped hold what was now the boy in. She never turned the key.

And then one afternoon she turned the key. The hulk shifted and jerked beneath her. It coughed to life, as if clearing its throat for the horrible song that it was about to sing. A spire of fetid black smoke farted out from somewhere, filling the cab and making Hannah cough. Inside of her she felt the boy shift.

Hannah turned the ignition off. She could hear the repercussion go out long and become small in the incomplete distance.

A week later the boy came. Hannah took a taxi to the hospital because Evan wasn't sure where Danny had gone. After all that time of holding him so tightly in, she had had to force the boy out.

"Birth is just the first step in a life of letting go of a child," Bethany had told her with a sigh. "It's just the first step of a child wanting to get the hell away from you."

Three days later she came home with the boy, with a wriggling pink grump of a thing. And all around was activity. The machines had come back to life. In the dirt fields the disembodied gullets gorged. The builders were building. Hannah was stuck at home with the boy, stuck there among the grumbling of the yellow herds and the hammering of the sun-browned men. Hannah let the men in to use the bathroom. They felt no need to hold it in around her. They passed through, tipping their hard hats, grinning at Hannah. Some of the older workers hovered over the boy, made faces at him. "We're short a guy today," one of them joked. "Mind if we borrow this one here?"

"You can keep him," Hannah joked back. Had she not had the boy there, her conversations with the men would have been flirting. With the boy, they were just adults being adults.

Danny didn't seem to know what to do with the boy. "I don't think he likes me very much," Danny admitted. The boy would cry and writhe whenever Danny picked him up, or made a move to pick him up.

"Of course he likes you, Dan. You're his father." As soon as she had said it, she realized that that made no sense. There were no promises.

He would stare at the boy, like he was trying to figure out what it was. One night she found Danny hovering over the crib. Hannah put her hand on Danny's back and her chin on his shoulder, kissed his cheek. It felt fully like a family to Hannah, until Danny spoke. "What celebrity would do his voice in one of those baby voice-over movies, do you think?"

They stared together at the sleeping baby, Hannah slowly removing herself from Danny.

"Orson Welles is dead, right?"

In three weeks there was another house just like Hannah's and Danny's and the boy's. In a week there were two more. By the time the boy had enough hand-eye coordination to hit Hannah on purpose, nowhere had become somewhere. And then someone started smashing all this glass in the street.

In the silence now, the music began again, like someone had turned a key. It bellowed and it screeched, a wailing rumpus. The boy cupped his hands to his ears and made a humdinger of a face with his fat. And then the key was taken out and there was quiet again. And there is no place more quiet than where noise has just been. But the boy kept his ears cupped, not trusting that it was done, not trusting that there wouldn't be more.

The garage door was open and the boys in the Fancy Dans faced out to the street, pretending they had an audience. Hannah waited at the bottom of the raked driveway, waited there with all the glass. The boy kept his ears cupped. The guitars squealed like one car scraping against another trying to park, the drums thumped insistently. Hannah could imagine that in their imaginations this was all spectacular. She had never particularly liked Bastard Hymns. They hadn't been very good, which was why they never went anywhere—not, as Danny always suggested, because it was all who you knew. But Hannah had loved watching them practice, loved watching them love every minute of playing their derivative songs, each the star of his own music video.

To be polite, she waited for the song to finish. Then Hannah would go to them, maybe tap a little applause. "Sounding good, guys," she could say. Hannah wouldn't ask them to quit it with the music, she would just ask about

Danny. "I don't suppose you boys have seen my husband?" But for now she waited for them to finish, there at the end of the driveway, at the spot where parents wait for their trick-or-treating kids. But the fracas kept running forward. First the vocals stopped, then the guitars, and then the bass, until it was just the drums.

Hannah climbed the drive and looked in. The boy followed behind her, squeezing the sides of his head like he was trying to crush it. Hannah looked in and the boy butted her in the bum. Hannah felt for him with her hand as she looked into the garage, and he bit her. Was this the wonder everyone kept talking about?

The rest of the band was standing dumbly around the garage, looking at Danny soloing. Hunched over, his belly was round like a kick drum. He had taken his shirt off and his whole body was pink and slick from exertion, slick like that one time they had disastrously tried oils. Danny's eyes were closed, his tongue sticking out the side of his mouth. This was the drumming face that he was so self-conscious of, the one that Hannah had loved instantly, found so damned dear. His bald spot beamed red. The Fancy Dans looked at him through the shaggy curtains of their hair, their instruments hanging off of them.

Danny looked like a plate spinner trying to keep everything moving. He worried around the kit, hitting everything in his way. He was big behind the sparkly red set meant for a kid. The kid who probably owned it waited on the steps to the house, drinking pop from a bottle. There was joy there on Danny's face, unbridled. He finished his solo by whacking at the cymbals. He would be so embarrassed, Hannah knew, if he could see his face right now, if he could see how cute and absurd he looked.

Throwing the sticks away with his final slam on the cymbals, Danny thrust his arms triumphantly in the air. Thrust his arms upward like he was trying to take off. But as much as he pumped he just could not get off the ground, weighed down like he was.

"That's it!" he yipped.

"That's it!" Danny whooped.

"That's it!" Danny pointed at the boys. His voice broke. "That's how you friggin *play* it!"

Comfortable that the noise was through, the boy uncupped his ears and reached out for his mother's hand. Hannah looked at Danny, watched him scream what it was. Feeling his fingers on hers, she let her hand unfold. Stealing the marble back, the boy broke for the street. Hannah turned from Danny and watched her boy's escape. Slow and determined, he waddled down the driveway, towards all that glittering glass that someone had either just started smashing or just stopped cleaning up. Momentum started to overtake ability, the boy started to tilt further forward, and Hannah knew how it would turn out. And, knowing that, what point was there in lunging to stop it?

# THE THING ABOUT THINGS

"Extra, Erma," I stress, reaching and feeling around inside of myself for the ability to be pleasant and patient with Erma.

"Extra," again, and I waggle the regular-large cup in her face. A half-hour before I sent her to the stockroom to fetch a stack more so the morning shift would be fully stocked for breakfast tomorrow. But I can smell the smoke break so acutely on her that she may as well have bull bursts fuming out of her nostrils. There even seems to be this fresh patina of nicotine on her skinny, wobbly teeth that somehow must have started out bright and clean and white once.

I'm waggling this cup I need in front of Erma's face until I get the focus of the dull fish swimming in the bowls of her eyes, then I fit an extra-large cup into that regular so that the lip of the extra sits up from the lip of the normal. With my fingers I make a pinch of the difference and hold that gap up for her to make the difference extra-clear, but also to kind of say This is how much patience I have left for you, Erma.

"*Extra.*"

Wiping down a table in Section 3, Lorrie looks up and gives a tired, sympathetic smile for me. More like for the situation than for me.

"Okay," Erma agrees, nodding at me as if the problem's one of semantics, or it's a philosophical quandary, and not just that she was smoking out back all that time and forgot what she was supposed to grab exactly. Mind settled, she staggers to the stockroom with the two cups to take another crack at it. But she'll just end up having another smoke, like she always does. And then she'll fall asleep in the stockroom, like she always does, until I come wake her up after close to take her home, like I always do.

I shrug my shoulders for Lorrie to see like What can I do? and she shrugs back like What can any of us do?

You can't help but talk to Erma like she's foreign. She's not, of course, but she also basically is. Because she's so, so old that she's practically from another time that may as well constitute a whole other country with a whole other language. And Erma's not even the only citizen of the Republic Of Old And Out Of It we've got. There's a baseball team's worth of blue hairs who run breakfast and who move at the same befuddled, disinterested pace, except they keep to the day shift, which is out of my jurisdiction. If Erma was any other old lady off the street working the 3-to-close shift I would have shit-canned her before you could say "Canada Pension," except Erma's not just any old lady. She's the boss's mom is the thing.

As a matter of policy we're expected to call this Place a Restaurant, but we're a Fast Food Joint, or simply a Place. The owner, J.R., has been working at this same Place since he was fourteen, the same age I was when I started. He climbed the ladder from mop jockey to owner, and he seems out to chart a similar trajectory for me. Because misery loves company is the thing. And J.R. loves me. I'm reliable and I'm a hard worker, but more than those things he trusts that I'd never breathe a word to his wife or to anyone else about the shit he talks to me about, the things he has in his head. Like this one night he called me into the back office during the thick of an unexpected after-supper rush just to bounce the benefits of making it with younger girls off of me. "If there's grass on the field," he assured me after some chin scratching, "I'll play." He'd apparently given the matter a lot of thought. Then he started wondering out loud about diddling old ladies, and said that he never did like playing ball on a snowy field but then admitted that sometimes a game of pick-up could be fun at just the right time, when you don't mind soaked clothes and frozen hands you can't even handle the ball with, and being dragged around through the snow so much that you start to get muddy as well as snowy, and then he forgot we were talking about pubic hair altogether and we wound up discussing football for fifteen more minutes. Up front, the girls got inundated and fell behind.

So it came as no big surprise that when J.R.'s father kicked it from this lung thing he had, mine was the lap into which he dropped his freshly widowed mother. And that's who Erma is.

"I don't think she's hardly slept since Dad died," J.R. was complaining to me the few days before he figured out to hire her. "All she does is sit around smoking and scratching lottery tickets." He said that she's up all night doing that, and spying on her neighbours, too. Erma phones J.R. at any hour to report what her Chinese neighbours are doing in their backyard. They go swimming and set off fireworks, the Chinese people, and Erma doesn't like that. J.R. described to me this thing that Erma described to him where the Chinese people light toilet paper on fire and make these long wriggling snakes of flame in the air, which actually sounds fairly awesome. All the while they're laughing. "And Mom hates the sound of their laughing because she doesn't know what they're laughing about. Chinese-y things, she says." He was going nuts until he figured out that he could keep her busy and out of his hair by making me busier and tangling her up in mine. He gave his eighty-one-year-old mother a job on the supper shift.

"Let me know about whatever she eats or steals," was all the instruction I got from J.R. Not a word about whether or not she was actually expected to do work like the rest of us. And not even the beginning of a hint about what I was supposed to do about her disappearing acts or her chronic smoking or her incessant napping. If Erma's eight-hour shift was a whole pie, it would be cut up into only two pieces: sleeping and smoking. The actual work Erma does is the crumbs left over in the tin and all over the table after the thing gets wolfed.

When she's slugging about and dropping off the face of the earth, and I'm ready to have kittens on her, I have to stop and remind myself of Erma's deal. I look at her and see this pathetic munchkin of a thing, all humped-over and small, with all these deep, deep creases running over whatever flesh she's got exposed like grey, hairy tree bark, and these big, hazy, empty eyes the colour of faded jeans where there's a yellow now to the almost white blue, bulbous behind lenses that are about as thick as the difference between large and extra-large cups. I look at Erma looking like that and it takes all the imagination and sympathy I've got to remind myself that underneath that gross husk are probably feelings. Or things like feelings. To keep from losing it on her, I have to remind myself that life must not be very good or very easy for Erma right now, to have lost her husband like that, and to have been sloughed off by her son like that. And to be working here, at this Place. At least we have that one burden in common.

All of this Erma stuff could have been worse. The old lady was one more hassle I didn't need, but when your job is nothing but a cobbling together of hideous, pointless hassles, one more is not that remarkable a thing. Like I imagine if I were to be shot with a machine gun, only the first few shots would hurt and then the rest would just be force without pain. But then Erma and the night bus driver got into some major spat. Something about Erma smoking on the bus and then howling all these racist invectives at the guy when he was telling her to stub it out, which is hard to imagine her doing, seeing as she has said hardly more than Okay and Yes and Extra to me all this time working together. Now none of the buses in the city will stop for her and it's fallen to me to drive her home nights after work.

And that's the thing about things. They could always be worse. All this Erma stuff is just regular-shitty and so who knows what extra-shitty actually looks like. Like even when things actually do get worse, you always say Oh, but they could always be worse, which is what you said last time. Which just means that you've gotten used to the way things have been since they did get worse. The worse gathers and piles up, but you just accustom yourself to it, I guess. Or else you just forget how good it used to be.

How much worse things would have to get for them to be extra-worse, frankly, is beyond me. I look at Erma—at and sometimes into those eyes with almost no colour in them at all—and wonder how well she might actually understand all that. All that extra.

When Lorrie mops she'll hunch over to scrub and down the V of her shirt you can make out the lines of ribcage beneath her freckly pink skin, like the rungs on a ladder that leads into the darkness and shadow of whatever else is down there, under her undershirt. She's putting up the chairs and mopping in what six years ago was the smoking section, trying to drop a hint to the old guy lingering there like we're a café. Two hours ago he ordered a cup of hot water and a kids' chicken nuggets. The nuggets are supposed to be in the shape of jungle animals, but they're really just humpy, knobby blobs of batter and are in the shape of elephants and lions and zebras like clouds are in the shape of anything. He has refilled his hot water three times and there is not two hours worth of news in that newspaper of his.

This guy is the guy that used to come in all the time with this other guy, The Captain. The Captain was this tall, hefty guy that had this stark pink line of scalp where his white hair parted to the side like the margin on notepaper. And he always had on pristine new sneakers that he would have been shot for in the ghetto back when that was happening. He was not decorated with any medals, and no sailing hat, and not much sign that his skin had ever been toughened under the sun on open water, but he was irrefutably The Captain. And it was just accepted that you were to treat him with this jovial reverence, and act vaguely subservient to him, and pour him a large club soda but only charge him for a small. When some new hire who didn't know would call him Sir—like Would you like fries with that, *sir*—everyone else would smirk, and The Captain would smirk, and that new guy would feel so completely alone without knowing why. Whoever the manager was would swoop in and apologize, saying how it's impossible to find good help these days like good help hasn't existed since the Captain's day, and The Captain would nod and wink, all assuaged and forgiving. Without ever being filled in, that new guy would catch on after a few visits and would adopt that same reverence like The Captain had saved his life once and they went way, way back.

So The Captain would come in here and command all this mysterious respect, and with him always would be this other guy. This is hot water and chicken nuggets guy. He didn't have a nickname and was treated just like any other old guy off the street. The two of them would sit across from each other, always at a window seat in what was then the smoking section, The Captain leaning back and staring off like in thought, and this other guy listing across the table like he was waiting to take notes of whatever The Captain said. They never did talk that I heard. The Captain would watch the parking lot and this other guy would just watch The Captain. The only indication that those two were at all friendly was when The Captain would drift away from his lot watch and make a little kissing motion and tap two fingers on his lips, and this chicken nuggets guy would pull out exactly two cigarettes from his breast pocket. Only hot water and chicken nuggets would smoke. The Captain just looked his smoke over, inspected it, tapped it thoughtfully on the table, and would eventually drift back to his perusal of the parking lot.

One day the bald guy came in without The Captain, got what he always got, sat alone and quiet for a few hours, took out his two smokes, smoked only one, left the other on the table, and then left. No one said anything. After years of this routine, after years of pretend respect and just the kind of intimacy there is in a shared joke or some shared secret—even if no one actually knew what the secret was—there was nothing. A part of me felt grieved and heavy, felt that someone should take the initiative to find out what had happened to The Captain, but this other part of me didn't care, and forgot about him altogether except when hot water and chicken nuggets comes in and all that rushes back like food I ate too quick.

It gets to eleven and I let Lorrie put up the chairs and put on the most grating music she has and dim all the lights but the ones directly above him and still this guy is flapping the paper like he's trying to get off the ground with it. Lorrie comes to me behind the counter. "You don't mind if I don't wait around all night for this guy to just keel over already, do you?" she asks me. She takes her cap off and tries her best to fluff her frizzy hair back into some presentable shape, but the top holds its dome.

Only a year shyer of thirty than I am, we started working at this Place around the same time and shared the same level of non-responsibility throughout high school. We would flirt and joke and would even get drunk together after work. We would get near to doing something together and being something together, always in the park adjacent to this Place where they've built a Canadian Tire now. But in her last year of high school she got caught up with some health or emotional something that she had never talked to me about and disappeared. Nine years later she came back to put herself through veterinary school and it was like she never knew me before. "Oh. You're still here," was about all she said. And we went from almost something to nearly nothing.

"Go ahead and take off," I tell her. "Me and Erma can finish everything up."

"Erma's still here?" Lorrie lifts her apron over her head

and there's the pink fish eye of her bellybutton. And fuzz. Lorrie came back without fifty pounds she couldn't afford and this real fine but also real prevalent hair all over her arms and her neck and her cheeks. The internet has all kinds of ideas about what this might mean.

"Around here somewhere."

"Well thanks, Ivan," she says, like my name could be a substitute for Mr. or Sir or Boss or Captain or any other name under the sun.

"Okay," is what I say.

Before giving hot water and chicken nuggets the boot I do my cash-out at the counter instead of the back office. Slapping the bills down like I'm dealing a deck of cards, letting him hear how put out I am, I stare at him shaking his paper there in what used to be the smoking section.

And this happens: looking at the guy, thinking about The Captain and about that area having been the smoking section, it's like I get sucker-punched in the gut. Because here is how time moves: time moves so automatically that it's basically like breathing. You don't pay attention until the wind gets knocked out of you, and then you feel and scrutinize every breath that you drag in and force out of yourself and along with the pain there is suddenly the something like pain that comes from focusing so tightly on a thing that you otherwise always take for granted.

Ruminating on those two old guys smoking in the smoking section, I start to think about back at the same time when Lorrie and I used to get along as easy as math on a calculator, and then about when the Canadian Tire was a park with climbers like dinosaur skeletons that we used to dangle from the ribs of wasted. And then here comes stupid remembrances of all the different coloured caps we've had since I've been here and from that comes the different ways J.R. has styled himself in a decade. When I started it was a ponytail and beard, which became a beard and a brush cut, and then a mustache and mullet, and then the same hair he has now except grey for a while and now it's been dyed this impossible brown since he's got his mistress and he's only got a plug of hair under his lip that he calls a flavour saver and that's disgusting. Thinking about him gets me thinking about me, about how I've only gained 10 pounds since starting at this Place but have somehow managed to get fat. At the start there were all these things I'd considered doing with my life, except there were too many things I half-wanted to do so I chose nothing instead of the wrong thing and so stuck around this Place until I decided, and how I've decided nothing. And I think about how things might have been different if Lorrie had stuck around, how if we weren't strong enough people on our own we might have added up to something that might have gone somewhere and done something, but now we're just who we are in the same Place we started anyway. All this from hot water and chicken nuggets.

Here's a fact: you can spend a week cleaning this Place from toe to head and still it would be filthy. From the meat sizzling on the grill and fries popping in the fryer this skin of grease has settled on every surface. I have to buy new sneakers every three months because this filth eats away at the rubber, exposing the honeycomb of bounce in the sole. Poolside rules apply around here: you don't dare rush or run because you'll for sure slip and crack your head wide open. I've seen it happen. Now, the work here has become so automated over time that the garbage bins have to be put in the exact same spot every night, otherwise you'll end up with a heap of wax burger squares on the floor beside the grill and the bunched up, sweaty plastic bags that the fries were in beside the fryer and turds of unwanted receipts on the floor beside the till. When you move these bins what you uncover are these sterling circles of tile that the grease hasn't been able to mar over all that time.

I pull up a chair, the seat across from the guy that used to be The Captain's. Hot water and chicken nuggets folds the paper in toward himself.

"It's past eleven," I say.

He flicks his wrist a few times like his watch is a Magic 8 ball and then squints at the time there, and then puts the thing to his ear. He looks back at his watch and stands up, giving one of those Erma nods, like the time is a matter of my opinion and not a fact up on the wall in plain sight.

"Well," he says, looking down on me, tapping the table. "Well," he says, "Time makes fools of us all."

Hot water and chicken nuggets folds the paper under his arm and I follow him to the door.

"Someone said that," he says as I open the door for him to leave out of.

I lock that door after him and stand there and watch him wander out alone into that dark, empty lot not overseen by any sort of Captain.

Erma's where I know she is, laid out dead to the world, spread over a few garbage bags of plush dinosaur dolls that we're giving away with the kids' meals, pillars of cups around her and a wall of jugs of fryer oil. J.R. is probably right about her not having slept regularly since his dad's death, the way Erma conks out like she does. Her whiskery, wrinkled mouth hangs open, her lids seem barely closed like she's not very deep in, and there's a sleeve of regular-large cups beside her on the floor.

"Erma," I say, pronouncing her name like I'm picking sides for teams.

"Okay," is what she says. She touches at her glasses to check that they're still there, and then touches her belly, to check that her cigarettes are still in her apron's pouch. Her eyes creep open like they're two small mouths too parched to ask for water.

Out back in the parking lot Lorrie is on the curb smoking and waiting for a ride still. Hunched over, I can make out the line of spine through her shirt, clear as the cut here dots on a coupon. Her hair still holds the shape of her cap.

Erma wobbles ahead of me and climbs into the car.

"Need a ride?" I ask Lorrie, locking up.

"No. They're coming for me."

"Want me to wait around until they show up?" I shake my keys in my hand like mixed nuts.

"That's fine. I'll be fine. Take off. Have a good weekend, Ivan."

"Okay," I say, agreeing with her in that Erma way because this is not fine and she will not be fine and I will not have a good weekend.

Three months into my working at that Place, J.R. calls me into his office for a sort of performance review. This was long before I was his best friend, back when he was still Mr. Roberts. He sits me down and what is it he says to me exactly?

He asks me out of the gate what my problem is, asks me why my work isn't getting done, and why it's getting done so slipshod when I actually do it. The pie that was my shift back then also had only two slices: flirting with the girls I worked with—the larger piece—and striving to be just vaguely insulting enough to the customers that they couldn't actually complain. And here's J.R. wanting me to account for the crumbs.

"Honestly?" I ask him.

"I'd rather you be," he says. "Saves me the trouble of having to sort through your shit."

"I don't care," I tell him flat out.

"And just what do you care about, Ivan?"

Not thinking about it, I'm pretending to, but I just stare at the calendar on the wall behind him, which has a picture of a different burger and combo for every month.

"Ivan," he says to me, sadly, after I don't answer, "Can I be honest with you?"

"Saves me the trouble of having to sort through your shit." Maybe this was the first time I made him smile.

"I don't care either," is what he finally says, laying his hands flat out on his ink blotter and letting his shoulders crumple. "I don't care, but, you know, I do it all the same. Because this is what I do. Pretending won't get you to the end, but it will get you pretty far. So, while I can't ask you to care, you can never make a person care, I can ask you that while I'm putting money in your pocket that you at least do me the solid of pretending that you do."

"Do the whole horrible world a favour," is what he says to me.

"Erma," I prod.

How the headlights gawk at her dark house makes it feel like we're here to burgle the place. This is the house J.R. grew up in and it's a small, pointless house with a lawn that means nothing, that hasn't changed since it was built, that the world has grown past and changed around, and a house that students will probably move into and hang flags and sheets instead of curtains in the windows of not long after Erma leaves it or she dies in it.

"Erma," I jostle.

These two mason jars full of pungent, yellow, swirling smoke with a few holes poked in the top to let that dirty haze out is how I imagine Erma's lungs. Because after the fifteen-minute ride where she slept the whole time the car smells like she's snarfed a pack.

A cough either wakes her up or she wakes up and coughs.

My workdays now end with these as painful as they are awkward two or however many minutes where we just sit in Erma's driveway. First it's me waiting for Erma to wake up on her own cognizance, and then it's Erma's baby-dumb wonderment of having woken up in a place different than where she fell asleep, and then it's just us waiting for something to happen. We never look at each other, but just sit and stare forward like two cats taking a shit in the same box, waiting. I know what it is I wait for: for her to clear out so I can move on to something that even if it's nothing like poking my head into a few bars to see if anyone I know is around, or renting a movie, or just going home and starting back up a paused game and getting drunk enough to fall asleep. Even if it's dick-all I've got on my plate it's mountains more important than idling in an idling car with a groggy old idling woman. But what Erma holds onto in those two minutes—okay: there's always this datey air in the car like a gas leak that I can't put my finger on, as if Erma's waiting blithely but also kind of impatiently for me to make some goodnight move on her, to jump her arthritic bones, to get a good and thorough feel of her scales, to let the hairs on my chin make static sparks with the hairs on hers, or at least for me to do the gentlemanly thing of getting out and opening the door for her.

Of all the girls I've driven home it's true that none were women, and I don't even know what you'd call Erma. The only thing Erma has in common with all the girls I've driven home over the past nearly fifteen years is that Place. And you can put bunny ears on driven home if you want. It's grodier than the floors there to think of J.R. hiring new girls with me in mind, but at the same time there was never a moment when I was without a fruity-smelling little blond to train, with soft hairs on her arms that would curl and char when she got too close to the grill. But you bet all that driving home—with and without bunny ears—had to stop as soon as I became a boss. But the thing is that as soon I stopped dating Place girls, I basically sort of stopped dating altogether. J.R. had done all the work for me up to that point, and now I feel sometimes with girls like this domesticated animal released into the wild, expected to open his own cans of chow all of a sudden. I can't help but suspect that J.R. knew he was making me reliant on him. The best way to make an animal love you is to make it need you.

Erma opens the door to finally get out and the insides of the car light up. She's stopped by some thought that has her take the smoke she has ready in her mouth out and then closes the door shut again, bringing back the muddy darkness, and turns to me.

"The light in the kitchen has been out for weeks," she crows like it's a fact I should already be aware of. "And Ken left a fridge of beer if you want."

I don't want to set foot inside that house, but when you're old there's no such thing anymore as asking questions, and in Erma's foreign language there's no such word as please.

So, “Fine,” I say, and cut the engine.

I follow behind Erma through the front door and knuckle the foyer light switch, but no light comes on.

“And that one too,” Erma says from somewhere in the dark house ahead of me. “Bulbs’re above the fridge.”

Feeling my way along the walls, every bulb in the house is unresponsive, I find out, and flicking the switches I’m just some brain sending signals to a dead heart. “Erma?” I call out, but she only responds by closing a drawer in some room somewhere. The only working light I find is the pimple of a bulb in the fridge, which gives the room only the pathetic sort of light that comes out of a cave when someone’s gone in ahead of you. But it’s enough light for me to make some sense out of the cupboard just above and find out of something like twenty bulbs enough that don’t tinkle with a shake.

Condiments and beer is all Erma has. Having seen enough ketchup and mustard in a day, I take a beer. And a second for the road.

The colour in the kitchen for a second glitches from blue to yellow. The window above the sink stares down on Erma’s Chinese backyard neighbours. There’s a tame party going on out there. The strips of flame they’re responsible for light up the lighter’s face and of course their happy, drunk expression looks evil in that light. They’re down there all laughing about something, that’s for sure, and I can make out the bodies of darting children around the edge of the pool. If this is the spot where Erma snoops and reports to her son of course she assumes the worst, because whatever you’re watching happen always seems more sinister anyway when you’re watching it from a dark place.

I twist in the bulb and feel the first burn of working light on my fingertips.

Pipes vibrate and grumble from somewhere in the house that's a tap coming on. Working towards the water sound, I detour back into the foyer and bring light there, poke my head first into a closet and then through the door to the basement, where I screw in fresh light, and then the living room. A silver frost is settled all over the coffee table and in the strands of the carpet, along with an even finer, duller white-grey powder. Scattered over the tables and sticking out of the couch cushions are loser tickets. And ashtrays. Ashtrays overflowing and overflowed, yellow stubs doubled over like people in pain.

The walls in Erma's house are a dull buttery brown, but not one solid colour. The walls are the uneven, hazy colour of Erma's fencepost teeth, the colour of Erma's tired, empty eyes, the colour of her lungs as I see them. Probably these walls were once pristine white, or maybe some cheerier yellow, or at any rate some colour clean and new and they've been gradually painted over by years of smoking. Filth gathers so gradually you don't even notice.

Hanging over the couch there's the Roberts family, a big wide portrait of them. There's J.R. with ears sticking out like thumbs wanting a ride and his unruly hair obviously fixed in a rush, probably around the age that he started working at that place. It's him at the end of his life, when you think about it. Lording over his family there's newly dead Ken Roberts, looking forward like he's just recognized the camera guy as someone who'd done him wrong years ago. He's large and imposing and defeated and smiling because he was told to. J.R. and his dad are smiling, but they're obviously not happy. Erma's the one that's not smiling, sitting there in front of her boy and her man, there with a flowery knotted scarf around her already withered neck, her glasses as thick as if I'm running out of patience with her, Ken and J.R.'s hands resting like dead animals on either of her shoulders. And she has on her face that look of stern, detached pride that people have on their faces when they're holding up some wound or injury to be photographed. It's like it doesn't hurt as much when you're presenting it as a fact and not a feeling.

With one bulb left I call "Erma?" and get a sustained cough with tears in it back to follow down the hall to the door open there, which is the bedroom. Water's being run inside, I guess in the connected bathroom, and there's some porcelainy tinkling on the sink and cabinets being rolled open and shut.

Not wanting to stand up on the bed to change the ceiling fan bulb, I give her light enough to find her smokes in the middle of the night by and change the bedside lamp. The water stops and Erma comes out of the bathroom prepped for bed. Across the bed from me Erma is lit up in her nightgown and underneath the fabric the shadow of her body is in the shape of a woman's body in the way that those chicken nuggets are in the shapes of what they're supposed to be.

"That's the last," I tell her.

She takes off and folds her glasses and not magnified and now squinting in the light her eyes look like her original eyes have been ripped from their sockets, and these little bulbs there now are the weird, gnarled, staved-in way they healed.

"Then have a lie down," is what she says.

"Until I fall asleep," is what she says to me, or what she asks to me.

The weirder things she could be asking me are she could be asking me to take her to the tub and reach with one of those hand loofas the spotty, rotting places that she can't get to anymore. Or she could be asking me to administer some strange-smelling medicinal vagina cream, or she could be flat out asking me to make love to her like her husband used to. Or she could be with trembling hands pulling a gun from the bedside table's drawer explaining to me that every night she sits up with the mouth of that thing kissing her forehead goodnight because she came all this way, lived all this way, if only to see what was at the end of the road, and only found a dump of loneliness and rejection and losing lottery tickets where she supposed there would be a park or a lake or at least some nice view. But she's only asking me to lay down for a few minutes, on top of the covers, no closer to her than we just were in the car.

Except I'm already on the bed when I'm thinking about this, trying to answer for myself why I sat so agreeably down. Why I reached across her to turn out the light.

She sparks a cigarette in the dark and her face lights up and as near as I can tell she takes only a lung full like it's a last breath before diving to the bottom of a pool, and then she puts the thing in the ashtray to let it burn like a stick of incense.

"I got so used to him," she whispers after us lying quiet for a while, her voice sounding like it's coming from in her chest. "I got so used to that fatso taking up all the room. You live long enough," and she here yawns with the whine of a dog yawning, "You realize that the only thing you can rely on is those goddamn annoying things. They somehow make life... Okay."

Only she says Okay in her way of agreeing only to get me to stop talking to her, and not Okay like Okay, fine, I think. Ken's beer's gone flat enough to drink the rest of the can easy.

One night after work and after 40s for both of us I was lying wasted next to Lorrie in that park where the Canadian Tire is now, us angled towards each other so that only our shoulders touched barely and our heads touched even more barely, and I became aware the way you become aware of things when you're newly drunk like that that something had to happen right then. It just came to me that if anything was ever going to happen between her and me it would have to be then, and it would have to be nudged into action by me. And what I did was I didn't do anything. There were these dark things swooping all over the sky and I wondered what sort of bird would be out that late until I realized they were bats, and instead of moving one inch towards her, or reaching out and simply dropping my hand on top of hers, I just watched those bats, listened to their weird chirping. And we lay for like an hour in that moment where something has to happen, we just lay there in that, at least I did, and what I'm realizing now is that who knows where Lorrie's head and heart was about all that stuff going on between us. Either she was completely into it and that explains why she's so cold to me now, because I didn't do anything and she blames my not doing anything for the way her life went, or else she was completely out of it and that explains why she treats me like nothing. Whatever it was, we lay there with that discomfort, and we just got used to it. I got used to the pain of not doing anything because I decided without deciding that the pain of doing something might be more painful. For an hour we were splayed out, and then sure we hung out again still, but never the same way, and then she left, and then she came back. And now I can't put my finger on the difference between not caring and not being willing to take the lumps that come along with caring.

Breath comes into Erma like the melt of a milkshake being sucked through a straw clogged with still solid milkshake.

"Erma," I say. And then "Erma" again, to make sure she's asleep. The smoldering eye of her cigarette burning is the only light in the room.

Leaving her, I go to the fridge for another beer. Out the window the Chinese family have tossed in the towel, and now there are only streamers of reflected patio light waving on the pool's surface and what's either a fat cat or a raccoon pawing at those wiggles. Watching the thing work, I empty that second beer and decide on another and then a few more just in case.

Put up on the fridge with a campaign magnet for Pierre Elliott Trudeau there's a yellowed black and white picture of Erma and Ken standing in some driveway at hardly twenty I bet. Ken is clutching his beefy arm around Erma, who poses for the shot with that same frank look of injury on her face from the family portrait. I want to decide if she was ever attractive so I take the picture off the fridge for a closer peek. Where the magnet was there's a perfect, full white sun high in the tea-stained sky and where the picture had been is a perfect white square on the fridge. The fridge is the colour of phlegm spat up by someone who's smoked their whole life, and right in the middle of it is this clean, untouched plot of healthy white.

I go and from over the couch I lift the Roberts family off their hook, which is like pulling the blinds or parting the curtains or lifting the flag and letting the day in because underneath the picture is this long rectangle of bright new wallpaper like a picture window. Here's the same coral colour that J.R. must have lived in as a boy, that got murky and dull along with him as he grew older. And somehow the light I let in through this window shines on how filthy Erma's living room is, like daylight will show the dust over everything, and the screen of mote always in the air, and the texture of grime over everything.

In the light of that day, and with whatever buzz of the beer I've already drank, I start to tidy up the living room, the mess so obvious now it's impossible to just leave. Mostly this cleaning up is just gathering up all the butts and pitching them and collecting all of Erma's loser cards. Opening another beer, I sit down on the couch with that stack of all different games, and with a dime double-check Erma's work. And I think about going through the whole house with this dime, scratching at the walls with it. Erma's missed boxes on every card, and while not all of these reveal a win some of them do, and by the dregs of the last of who knows how many of dead Ken's beers I've killed I've won Erma sixty dollars. Not exactly enough for her to retire from the fast food industry, not exactly enough to escape that Place, but nothing to wag a stick at.

At this point too wasted to drive home, I try to pass out on the couch. When that doesn't take, I stumble back to where I left Erma. Behind me as I go I turn out all the lights.

I'd say Erma looks dead, only I've never seen a dead thing to compare to how Erma looks lying in the bed. She looks unoccupied—no lights on inside. From the racket of her breathing, though, I can say for sure that she's not at all dead. Standing in the doorway, considering the big empty spot beside her, I listen to her painful-sounding shallow gurgle. As horrible as it all sounds, it at least lets me know that she's still alive, which is something.

# I'M SORRY AND THANK YOU

He came out onto his porch and there was some hippy mother changing her baby on his lawn. On a Hudson Bay blanket the mother was wiping and dabbing at the muddy rolls and creases of her little girl. A gust of wind whipped up leaves around the two, and it was like last night on TV. Some pear-shaped Spanish grandma had been crammed into this glass booth with money going nuts all around her. The grandma had grabbed at the bills, stuffing her clothes with money, this twisted look of desperation on her leathery face. She had looked so stupid. He couldn't tell if the point was to degrade the grandma, but he could tell that this grandma didn't care. When the wind in the booth was turned off all the money dropped and lay in a pile at her feet. All that money just right there, but not for her. She had gotten some, but not enough. Never enough. Not quite like money, brittle and wet leaves stuck to the felt of the hippy mother's dreadlocks and onto the swamp of the little girl.

"I'll just be a sec," the hippy mother said when she saw him there on the porch. He took a sip from his mug and nodded, slid a hand into the pocket of his housecoat as a sign of being a-okay with things.

The hippy mother stood up with a bundle in her hand and walked to him. The baby writhed on the blanket like it was trying to crawl along the air.

"Hi," the hippy mother said. She had one of those cute, tired, hippy-dippy faces that would have been ugly if she had tried to pretty it up with make-up, he thought.

"Morning," he said.

The mother winced at the sun high above them and looked back at him, squinting still.

"Listen," she said, "I'm sorry to do this, but I've got nowhere to toss this." She held up the bundle. "I was wondering if you wouldn't mind taking it for me."

"That's shit in there?" he asked, gesturing at the bundle with his mug.

"Pretty much."

"I don't know why," he said, "but I always think that babies have those things that birds have. Now, what are those things called?"

The hippy mother didn't know.

"You know. It's that thing that birds have where they do a combination of shitting and peeing so you can't tell what the hell it is that's coming out. Just a bunch of disgusting stuff that doesn't make any sense. It's called *something*, what they have. It's like 'The Cloister,' only it's not. It's got *ache* in it somewhere I think." He shut his eyes tight and gritted his teeth, trying to force the word to the surface. "And it's right there, too."

"Fuck," he said, popping open his eyes. "It's frustrating, huh? When you can't think of a word you know. It's like having one of those sneezes where you can't sneeze. Do you ever get those?"

The hippy mother did get those. She was smiling still, but

it was a smile that didn't mean anything, like when a car in front of him would forget to turn a turn signal off.

"Do you mind if I just leave this here?" she asked, and anyway bent down and set the soiled bundle on the bottom step of his porch.

"Just so long as you don't set it on fire," he said, and laughed.

"Right. I promise not to," she said. "But thank you. And, again, I'm sorry. She already... And I was just going to... Anyway, I'm sorry and thank you."

She turned and walked back across the lawn, picking leaves out of her hair.

"Don't forget your baby," he called from the porch. He took another sip from his mug and made a surprised, sour baby face, expecting it to actually be coffee, forgetting about the Canadian Club. The only club he'd ever belonged to, his wife used to say. She had thought she was just a riot, that woman. Now, there was someone he'd like to cram into a booth. But not a booth with money. Maybe a booth full of razor blades or something. How easily could those become airborne?

"Got her, thanks," the mother said, gathering up her squirming girl.

He watched her put the kid into one of those hippy slings that he was starting to see regular people use now, too, and he watched her go, watched her bum as she went.

"Cloaca," he said.

"Cloaca!" he yelled. "It was the cloaca!" he yelled at her. Down the sidewalk, the hippy mother turned to look at him, then turned away and moved off a bit more swiftly.

"Cloaca," he said, feeling good, feeling like he had sneezed that sneeze out, or like he had suffered water in his ear all day from a swim and finally it was trickling out now, all hot and amazing.

"Cloaca," he said.

He had come out for the paper when he saw the shitty baby on his lawn. Now he squatted and sorted through the rolls that had built up by his door and found the one with the most recent date. All these people had died somewhere because of something, he read.

He picked out the business section, shook it out as he stepped down the steps of his porch, fluffed the paper, and then spread it next to the bundle the hippy mother had left him. With his bare toe, he nudged the wad of cloth onto the paper and wrapped it up.

He breathed in. There was the sweet and pungent smell, the complicated scent of baby shit. Any smell you miss, even if it's a bad one, is a good one.

Wadding the newspaper and the cloth full of shit into a ball the size of a softball, he walked to the end of the driveway, and then he threw it. The wad landed with a light heaviness onto his neighbour across the street's roof.

Opening his nostrils and opening his lungs, he hoped for that autumn smell, but still it was baby stench. He smelt his hands, but it was not his hands. It was all over the air now, that baby smell.

Another whirl of wind came and tossed the salad of dead leaves on his lawn. The leaves flirted around him, and he began to grab at them. He snatched all he could out of the air, stuffing them into the pockets of his bathrobe, and then into his robe so they scratched his bare chest.

The wind died and he stood there with the heap at his feet, his pockets full and his chest bulky. A leaf had landed in his mug. He could drink around that.

"Cloaca," he said, feeling pretty okay about himself.

**ACKNOWLEDGMENTS**

If this book was a park bench, these names would be carved on there: Kelly Hopkins, Robbie MacGregor, Nicholas Boshart, Anna Leventhal, Megan Fildes, Chloe Vice, Jenner Berger, Brad de Roo, Dan "The Boy" Mancini, Claire Turner Reid, Emily LaBarge, Michael Lista, Gregory John Morrell, Ross Lyle, Tara Kuhn, Dawn Matheson, Peter Henderson, Peter Coleman, Dan Evans, The Bookshelf, Trevor Ferguson, Simon Dardick, Andrew Steinmetz, Martha Magor, Emily Schultz, Shane Neilson and Caryl Peters, Drew Nelles, Jeff Stautz, David McGimpsy, Stewart Ross, and the Canada Council for the Arts. And, all in one big heart, MomDadMattMeganMiles.

And if this book was a park bench, Timothy Marcus Miller Kramer would be the man who takes a seat beside you, even though there are plenty of other free benches down the way. He chuckles to himself and you ignore him. And then he laughs again and you ask, "Say, what's so funny?" Not looking at you, he sighs wistfully and says, "Oh, nothing. Just the horror of being alive."

**INVISIBLE PUBLISHING** is committed to working with writers who might not ordinarily be published and distributed commercially. We work exclusively with emerging and under-published authors to produce entertaining, affordable books.

We believe that books are meant to be enjoyed by everyone and that sharing our stories is important. In an effort to ensure that books never become a luxury, we do all that we can to make our books more accessible.

We are collectively organized and our production processes are transparent. At Invisible, publishers and authors recognize a commitment to one another, and to the development of communities which can sustain and encourage storytellers.

If you'd like to know more please get in touch.
info@invisiblepublishing.com

Invisible Publishing
Halifax & Toronto